PRAISE FOR
THE MRS. MURPHY SERIES

SNEAKY PIE FOR PRESIDENT

"A deft combination of entertainment and education, Brown's latest will resonate with anyone concerned about the future of the nation—and the world."
—*Richmond Times-Dispatch*

"There are many election-related books you could choose to help you endure the final months of the presidential race, from desk-pounding policy proposals to thick, shelf-crushing biographies. Or, you could turn to *Sneaky Pie*."
—NPR

THE BIG CAT NAP

"A charming and enchanting mystery that affirms the Crozet cozies remain fun tales as Harry and her Puss 'n Cahoots squad investigate the homicides. . . . Fans will appreciate this engaging anthropomorphic whodunit."
—Futures Mystery Anthology Magazine

"Top honors go to the author's love for her beloved Virginia countryside and for her animal characters, who as usual steal the show."
—*Kirkus Reviews*

"A welcome return to cozy form . . . Amusing exchanges among the cats and dog and their commentary on the humans around them will please series fans."

—*Publishers Weekly*

HISS OF DEATH

"[Rita Mae] Brown ratchets up the tension in a conclusion that brings Harry, the killer, both cats, the dog and two horses into the final showdown. Brown . . . reunites the reader with beloved characters, supplies a wealth of local color and creates a killer whose identity and crimes are shocking (in one case, particularly so)."

—*Richmond Times- Dispatch*

"As explained on the book's cover, it takes a cat to write the purr-fect mystery. Indeed . . . With a baffling mystery at hand (or paw), it might just prove to be one of [Harry's] most perplexing cases."

—*Tucson Citizen*

"Brown sensitively depicts Harry's cancer treatment as the paw-biting action . . . builds to the revelation of a surprising killer."

—*Publishers Weekly*

CAT OF THE CENTURY

"[Rita Mae Brown's] animals are as witty as ever."
—*Kirkus Reviews*

"There are plenty of suspects with motives in a well-constructed cozy that readers will enjoy in this one sitting read."
—The Mystery Gazette

"The mystery part of *Cat of the Century* is quite good. The clues are there but the reader is still left guessing."
—Jandy's Reading Room

SANTA CLAWED

"Fun and satisfying. . . . An essential purchase for all mystery collections."
—*Booklist*

"[A] whodunit . . . that fans of the furry detectives and their two-legged pals will appreciate."
—*Publishers Weekly*

"Fearless feline and clever canine sleuths."
—*Kirkus Reviews*

"For all mystery collections and essential for series fans."
—*Library Journal*

"Captivating . . . will keep readers guessing who-dunit to the very end. A delightful Christmas present indeed."
—*The Free Lance-Star*

"Anyone who's a sucker for talking animals or who simply enjoys fantasizing about the thoughts running through a beloved pet's brain will find heaps of guilty pleasure in Brown's latest addition to the Mrs. Murphy series."
—*Rocky Mountain News*

"The animals once again provide . . . the best comic moments."
—*Alfred Hitchcock's Mystery Magazine*

"[A] satisfying whodunit with a wealth of Virginia color. And, as always, the real fun comes from Tee Tucker, Mrs. Murphy and Pewter. . . . In *Santa Clawed*, they're the true Christmas angels."
—*Richmond Times-Dispatch*

THE PURRFECT MURDER

"Brown provides a perfect diversion for a cold night, complete with a cat or a dog on your lap."
—*Richmond Times-Dispatch*

"Veteran readers . . . will not be disappointed in this outing."
—*Winston-Salem Journal*

"The well-paced plot builds to an unpredictable and complex conclusion."
—*Publishers Weekly*

"The pets steal the limelight . . . [and] offer pleasure to fans of animal sleuths."
—*Kirkus Reviews*

"The plot moves easily and those non-humans who speak to each other, if not to their people, are a real pleasure and well worth one's time."
—iloveamystery.com

PUSS 'N CAHOOTS

"Such a delight to read."
—*Albuquerque Journal*

"The novel's tight pacing, combined with intriguing local color, make this mystery a blue-ribbon winner."
—*Publishers Weekly*

"This clever mystery strikes a comfortable balance between suspense and silliness."
—*Booklist*

"Fans of the cunning animal sleuths will enjoy their antics and the spot-on descriptions of the horse-show circuit."
—*Kirkus Reviews*

"[Rita Mae Brown has] readers guessing whodunit until the very end."
—*The Free Lance-Star*

SOUR PUSS

"*Sour Puss* makes for a sweet read. . . . Brown has a devilish sense of humor."
—*The Free Lance-Star*

"One of my all-time favorite cozy series . . . This series is just plain charming."
—*The Kingston Observer*

"[The authors] have once again pounced upon just the right ideas to keep this delightful mystery series as fresh as catnip in spring. . . . These are books written about and for animal lovers. . . . One of the best books in a good series, *Sour Puss* should leave fans purring."
—*Winston-Salem Journal*

"A captivating look at grape growing and the passionate dedication it requires."
—*Publishers Weekly*

"This venerable mystery series has been on a good run of late. Brown does everything right here. . . . Wine fanciers or not, readers will happily toast the animal-loving author for creating this robust and flavorful tale."
—*Booklist*

CAT'S EYEWITNESS

"Thirteen is good luck for the writing team of Rita Mae Brown and her cat Sneaky Pie—and for their many fans. The Browns know how to keep a mystery series fresh and fun."
—*Winston-Salem Journal*

"This mystery, more than the others, has depth—more character development, a more intricate plot, greater exploration of the big topics. I give it nine out of ten stars."
—*Chicago Free Press*

"This book could not have arrived at a better time, the day before a snowstorm, so I had the perfect excuse to curl up by the fire and devour *Cat's Eyewitness* virtually at a sitting. . . . Entertaining, just the thing for a snowy afternoon . . . well worth reading."
—*The Roanoke Times*

"It is always a pleasure to read a book starring Harry and Mrs. Murphy but *Cat's Eyewitness* is particularly good. . . . Rita Mae Brown delights her fans with this fantastic feline mystery."
—*Midwest Book Review*

"It's terrific like all those that preceded it. . . . Brew the tea, get cozy, and enjoy. This series is altogether delightful."
—*The Kingston Observer*

"Another winsome tale of endearing talking animals and fallible, occasionally homicidal humans."
—*Publishers Weekly*

"The gang from Crozet, Virginia, is back in a book that really advances the lives of the characters. . . . Readers of this series will be interested in the developments, and will anxiously be awaiting the next installment, as is this reader."
—*Deadly Pleasures Mystery Magazine*

"An intriguing new adventure . . . suspenseful . . . Brown comes into her own here; never has she seemed more comfortable with her characters."
—*Booklist*

"Another fabulous tale . . . wonderful . . . The book is delightful and vastly entertaining with a tightly created mystery."
—*Old Book Barn Gazette*

"Undoubtedly one of the best books of the Mrs. Murphy series . . . a satisfying read."
—Florence *Times Daily*

SNEAKY PIE
FOR PRESIDENT

A Novel

RITA MAE BROWN &
SNEAKY PIE BROWN

ILLUSTRATED BY MICHAEL GELLATLY

BANTAM BOOKS NEW YORK

2013 Bantam Books Mass Market Edition

Copyright © 2012 by American Artists, Inc.
Illustrations copyright © 2012 by Michael Gellatly
Excerpt from *The Litter of the Law* by Rita Mae Brown copyright © 2013 by American Artists, Inc.

Published in the United States by Bantam Books, an imprint of The Random House Publishing Group, a division of Random House, Inc., New York.

BANTAM BOOKS and the HOUSE colophon are registered trademarks of Random House, Inc.

Originally published in hardcover in the United States by Bantam Books, an imprint of The Random House Publishing Group, a division of Random House, Inc., in 2012.

ISBN 978-0-345-53047-9
eBook ISBN 978-0-345-53354-8

This book contains an excerpt from *The Litter of the Law* by Rita Mae Brown. This excerpt has been set for this edition only and may not reflect the final content of the forthcoming edition.

Cover design and illustrations: Beverly Leung
Cover illustrations include images © Daniel Pelvin (cat silhouette), © Mike McDonald/Shutterstock (front cover button motif), © zentilia/Shutterstock (back-cover bottom left button), © Terri Francis/Shutterstock (back-cover upper left button)

Printed in the United States of America

www.bantambooks.com

9 8 7 6 5 4 3 2 1

Bantam Books mass market edition: August 2013

In honor of the
Montblanc Diplomat.
Perfection. Pure and Simple.

"The greatness of a nation and its moral progress can be judged by the way its animals are treated."

—Mahatma Gandhi

A Note from the Author

From a writer's perspective, the line between fact and fiction is considerably less clear than most readers realize.

To illustrate my point, I'll provide an example. Naturally, I am the star of the book you are about to read, but this very important tome also features (in much less important roles) the fat cat Pewter and the wise corgi Tucker—both of whom will be familiar to readers of my bestselling Mrs. Murphy mystery series showcasing the misadventures of a hapless human called Harry Haristeen. Neither Mrs. Murphy nor Harry show up here but, no big surprise, another human intrudes in these pages now and then.

You have never before met Tally, a Jack Russell featured herein, whom I live with in real life. I do not include her in the mysteries. She's enough trouble as it is. The Human referred to throughout is my co-writer, Rita Mae Brown. In truth, her role as co-writer is a minor one, in that she merely writes down what I say—but it's unlike me to denigrate her publicly, discretion being the better part of valor. (She gets cranky and then there are less treats for all. Also, she takes care of mailings so I must tread oh-so-carefully.)

Now, on to more important matters, like saving the planet!

Vote for me!

SNEAKY PIE
FOR PRESIDENT

CHAPTER 1

A United Front, with Tails

" 'When in the Course of human events.' " Sneaky Pie took a breath. The cat paused in her reciting. "There's the fatal flaw right there! *Human*. The Declaration of Independence limits itself to a species that has weak senses and is highly irrational."

"Well, there's nothing we can do about it," Pewter replied to the sleek tiger cat. She had just found the perfect spot of sunlight to relax in. "Why get worked up over it?"

But the gray cat's political apathy did not at all slow down the now-worked-up Sneaky Pie. "Leave these humans to their own devices and eventually laws will be passed forcing us to wear clothes."

"You can't be serious." Pewter's voice rose sharply.

"Underpants?" Awakened by the talk, Tally, the

Jack Russell, roused herself. "Underpants. I'm not wearing underpants."

"Oh, I can see you now, a lovely floral pair of silk panties with precious lace." Pewter licked her lips, a hint of malice enlivening her face.

"Panties! Panties! Never." The pint-sized dynamo ran in circles as if chasing her tail.

"Sit down, idiot," Tee Tucker, the corgi, commanded her housemate.

"I am not an idiot." Tally sat, but not before baring her impressive white fangs.

"Dogs forced to wear silly outfits is not so farfetched," said Sneaky Pie. "You've listened to the presidential debates. One Bible-thumping fellow thinks if gay marriage is passed, humans will want to marry animals. Making us wear clothes might just be the next step after that." Sneaky imagined the future with such a president.

"Gross!" Pewter spat out.

"Sex. Sex. Sex!" Tally jumped up, running in circles again.

"Sit down, for Christ's sake. You're making me dizzy," Tucker again commanded.

"Underpants, sex." The pretty little rough-coated Jack Russell raised her eyebrows. "This is just too weird."

"That's my point." Sneaky Pie walked over to

the distressed dog. "If a human running for president wastes everyone's time yammering about deviant sex, politics has gone truly off the rails."

"Zoom!" Tucker moved her head as though watching a speeding train, lowering her voice. She asked her three friend animals, "Have you had deviant sex?"

Sneaky Pie swatted her right on the rump. "Of course not! Among us, let's raise the tone, please!"

"Sex! Sex! Sex!" Tally shrieked in opposition.

"Will you sit down!" Both cats shouted at the young unspayed female dog.

Tears came to Tally's soft brown eyes. "I don't want to wear frilly underpants. What can we do?"

"How about a Declaration of Independence for animals?" Pewter sensibly suggested. "People revere Thomas Jefferson's writing on humans' so-called unalienable rights, or they pretend to do so, anyway."

"*Pretend* is the operative word. Believe me, if he came back and tried to run as a candidate today, they'd throw him out of Convention Hall," Tucker declared.

"Back to my original thought, there's nothing we can do about it," said Pewter.

"Pewts, if these humans destroy their political

system, it's going to affect us one way or the other. We are Americats, after all."

Tally jumped up in excitement, then sat right back down when she noticed all the others giving her the evil eye. "I'm an Ameridog."

"Doesn't sound as cool," Pewter scoffed, casually licking her front paw.

"Still counts." Tally took on a belligerent tone.

"She's right. We're all Americans." Tucker seconded Tally.

"Yes, you are," Sneaky conceded. "Okay, the clothing and sex sickness among humans is bad enough. Even worse, their drilling, logging, mining could wipe out where we live. Chemicals, especially from some kinds of mining, leak into the soil, then into the water supply. It doesn't look good."

"Logging's okay," said Tally, now sitting herself next to Pewter, then leaning on the large cat. "You can always grow more trees."

"Tally's right again." Tucker sought to praise the excitable dog.

"Perhaps," said Sneaky, "but humans cutting trees must be careful. They can't just buzz-cut the world and leave slash all over the place."

"Roll the slash in rows and little animals can make homes there. You know, like bunnies. Then

I can hunt them." Pewter smiled broadly. "Besides, *our* own human manages timber."

Sneaky replied, "Yes, she's responsible about timbering, but that doesn't stop other humans from pouring sludge into the rivers. My point is, we can no longer allow them to run things."

Pewter enjoyed a life of leisure. She sighed. "Oh, please, why not? Politics is so boring. Let the humans do it."

"Us?" Tally was incredulous, looking at all the other animals before setting her gaze on Sneaky. "You think we should take control?"

"We couldn't do any worse." Sneaky laughed.

"Taxes? I'm not paying taxes," Tally petulantly declared. "I worked hard for my bones and I'm not giving them up."

"You share with me," Tucker replied.

"I live with you," Tally said. "And if I don't share, you'll steal when my back is turned."

"It's a smart dog that buries its bones," the older corgi said and laughed.

"A juicy deer bone is a juicy deer bone." Tally shrugged. "And I do share with you, Tucker, even if I don't really want to."

"I am appalled." Pewter turned her head away from the dog, got up, and sat with her back to Tally. "You don't share with me."

"What'd I do?" asked Tally.

"Told the truth," Sneaky Pie replied. "Nobody—not people, not animals—wants to hear that."

"You and I tell the truth to each other," said Tally.

A long silence followed this. "Sometimes we do," said Sneaky at last.

"What do you mean by that?" Tally asked, while Pewter sighed loudly for effect.

"I keep a lot to myself," Sneaky Pie said.

"I don't." The dog lay down, head on front paws.

"We know," the two cats and corgi said in unison.

"You all are making fun of me," said Tally.

"Who else are we going to make fun of?" Pewter turned around.

"How about our human?"

"Too easy." Pewter puffed out her gray chest. "She'd be dead if we weren't here to guide her. I mean, she doesn't have a grain of sense."

"She's not so bad." Tucker did love the person in the house, and would defend her to the death. "She gets sidetracked a lot."

"If she'd stop watching the debates and reading the paper, she'd be all right. She always gets this way during elections." Pewter thought the woman in their lives wasted a lot of time on nonessentials.

"She read aloud the Constitution to us the other night. What good is that to me?"

"We can use the Constitution as well as she can. I certainly value my free speech," the tiger cat replied.

"Oh, Sneaky, none of them has a clue as to what we're saying. It's all a big waste of time. Let's forget all this and see if we can open the cupboard door." The thought enlivened the gray cat. The dogs, too.

"She's put the fresh catnip in a tin," said Sneaky Pie. "Won't do any good."

"I could bite holes in the tin," Tally offered, mouth watering. She looked toward the kitchen.

"I'll pull out the little sack of Greenies, I can chew through the sack," Tucker added. "Maybe I can figure out a way to open the tin, too."

"*Smelling* catnip is better than no catnip at all." Pewter raced for the cupboard.

From the living room, Sneaky Pie heard the cupboard door open. Pewter could be clever with her claws. If a container didn't have a twist cap, that cat could usually figure out a way to open it.

Sneaky heard Pewter pull out the Greenies sack. Just as it hit the wooden kitchen floor with a thud, the back door opened.

"Head for the hills!" Pewter yelled.

Tucker blasted out of the kitchen, her tailless rump disappearing down the hall.

Tally, a step behind, turned. "It's okay. It's only Sid from FedEx."

Sure enough, the FedEx delivery man placed a small carton on the table by the back door, closed it, and left.

"Whew." Tucker headed back to the kitchen.

Sneaky joined the thieves there. "Sid makes me think. If you drive a truck, a car, you know the rules of the road. You have to memorize them. Once you have those rules in your head, you can drive and get anywhere you want. Drive in the right lane. Put on your turn signal if you're turning. Don't park at a fire hydrant. Makes perfect sense, and it works."

"So?" Pewter was more concerned with the tin of catnip Tally had in her jaws. "Get your fangs up under the crease of the lid."

"I'm trying." The little dog dropped the square tin, then Tucker snatched it up.

"If the other drivers aren't drunk, drugged out, or texting, everyone is okay," continued Sneaky Pie. "My point is, like the rules of the road, there should be rules for living together."

"That's a good one. Never happen." Pewter, on

the other side of the tin, was prying it with her claws.

"You two aren't listening to me, and this is important."

"Nothing is more important than catnip," Pewter passionately said.

"Greenies." Tally's bag rested right beside her.

She left the bag to help Tucker and Pewter.

The dog really was being a good egg, because she surely loved those Greenies.

"*Pfft*," Sneaky exhaled.

"One, two, three." Pewter counted as she, Tucker, and Tally bit and pulled hard. "Got it!"

"Pull the string on this sack," Tally told Pewter, the cat's face already in the catnip.

"Okay." The gray cat hooked the yellow string with one exposed claw and the bag opened just enough.

"You know when she gets home there will be hell to pay." Sneaky inhaled the enticing scent before diving into the catnip, now all over the floor.

"Make hay while the sun shines." Pewter succumbed to overwhelming bliss.

"That is so tired." Sneaky now put her nose in the small plant buds and stems broken into little pieces.

"Can you think of a better one?" Pewter challenged.

"No," she purred in reply.

"Never put off until tomorrow what you can do today," Tucker said.

Tally, with a Greenies bone sticking out of one side of her mouth, mumbled, "Too puritanical. Let the good times roll, I say."

The two cats' glassy eyes turned to her.

Tally laughed, dropping her bone for a moment. "Do it now. You're going to be dead a long time."

CHAPTER 2

Give Peace a Chance

"Isn't that the dumbest name, Tufted Titmouse?" Pewter giggled, looking up at the handsome little bird, the size of a sparrow.

"*Fatass* is funnier," the saucy bird called down from the thin branch of a loblolly pine. Below her, Pewter and Sneaky Pie strolled down a farm road, just west of where the human lived.

Sneaky Pie laughed. The gray cat smacked her.

"Hey!"

"Well, stop encouraging him," Pewter reprimanded Sneaky. "How quickly you forget."

"Forget what?"

"I was the one who liberated the catnip. You wimped out."

"I didn't wimp out."

13

"Yeah, sure. We didn't even get spanked for it. All she did was bitch and moan and sweep up what we left," Pewter boasted, quite satisfied with herself.

As the cats walked along the dirt road, woods on one side and open pasture on the left, other birds flocked to join the insulting Tufted Titmouse. Black-crested Titmice flew to perch on branches along with chickadees, creepers, and one Downy Woodpecker, all of them chattering away.

"Fatty, fatty," they called down, encouraged by Joe, the Tufted Titmouse.

Pewter was fuming. "I might just call all of you chickens. Fly off those branches and I'll kill every last one of you," she threatened.

A well-groomed chickadee flew lower and counseled the gray cat in a confidential tone. "If you ignore Joe, he'll pick on someone else."

The Tufted Titmouse overheard. "You are such a gossip," said Joe to the chickadee. "You try to get on the good side of everyone, woo them into telling you stuff, then you *chirp chirp chirp* it all over the woods, the fields, the farm."

Glynnis, the chickadee, who was indeed inclined to chirp too much, protested, "I am no gossip."

"Well, I have some gossip." Sneaky Pie sat down, wrapping her impressive, bushy tail around her.

"Really?" Above, on her perch, Glynnis was enthralled before she even heard a word.

"Do you really, really?" chirped the chickadee, excitedly swooping in circles.

"Really." Sneaky Pie nodded to the chickadee, then looked up at the other gathered birds, who now fell silent. "You know this is a presidential election year?"

"Of course we know," the Downy Woodpecker replied. "I hear all about it."

"You do?" The Black-crested Titmouse flew closer to the woodpecker, larger than he was but not huge like the Pileated Woodpecker.

"The radio in the barn, the radios in the trucks, and if you sit on the ledge of the open window you can hear everything on the TV. *Same old same old*," the woodpecker said, her voice a staccato.

A tinier-than-usual Yellow Warbler, just two years old, looked up to the Downy Woodpecker with wide eyes. "What's an election?"

The Downy cocked his head. "A bunch of people say hateful things about one another and then promise the moon to other people, who give them money. Whoever gets elected gets to live in a fancy house. They can eat all the seeds they want. It happens every few years, and humans fall for it every time."

"Oh, my." The Yellow Warbler shook her head, confused. "I'm afraid I don't understand."

"Do you want to hear my gossip or not?" The tiger cat swished the tip of her tail.

"Tell! Tell!" the chickadee begged.

The Tufted Titmouse dropped down to a lower branch as well. "I told you Glynnis lived for gossip."

"Oh. This is about the presidential election. If a Bible-thumper gets elected, your name will be changed."

"Joe. The Bible-thumper will outlaw the name Joe?" The Tufted Titmouse—whose name was Joe—was incredulous.

"No, he and his followers will outlaw any words they think salacious: words like *titmouse*." Sneaky pronounced this with gusto.

"Never!" both the Tufted and the Black-crested blurted out.

Pewter, catching on, baited the birds. "For these hormone-addled humans, I'm afraid your name possibly has a sexual connotation."

"What? My name? My *species* name?" Joe snapped his bill, which clicked. "Impossible."

"Nothing's impossible in an election year. Think it over," Sneaky calmly advised.

"Not only will the religious nuts change your

name, they are going to make Sneaky and me wear four little bras." Pewter gilded the lily.

At that, Glynnis laughed so hard she nearly fell off her perch. The cats might have had an early supper. .

Just then a cowbird who had been sitting on the pasture-side fence joined the avian group.

"Pickpocket!" the Yellow Warbler screamed. "Lazy! Bad mother!"

"Shut up, squirt." The cowbird glared at the tiny bird, who usually stayed high in the trees.

But the Yellow Warbler was indignant. Tiny, but indignant. It was something to see. "You lay an egg among mine, then leave me to feed and raise it. Your behavior is despicable."

"Yeah, well, I've seen you push them out. Splat!" the cowbird responded. "So stop acting so high and mighty."

"It's not my job to hatch your egg." Puffed up, small though she was, the Yellow Warbler did look tough.

"Do you really do that?" asked Pewter. It was hardly normal bird behavior to abandon eggs. But then the whole species was flighty. Pewter liked them for breakfast or lunch. . . .

"Well, why should I exhaust myself if someone else will do the work for me?" the cowbird defended herself. She was tired of this argument. It's like everyone wanted to give her mothering advice.

Sneaky, considering this, replied, "You don't care if your egg is destroyed?"

"Some make it, some don't," said the cowbird. "Anyway, I am not raising a bunch of brats, beaks always open, squawking for more food. Give me a break."

Still puffed up, the Yellow Warbler sharply added to the conversation. "You could stop breeding. Try and control your primal urges!"

"Why? As long as I can get away with it, this girl just wants to have fun."

Glynnis was reveling in the exchange. With a superior tone, she said, "The rest of us are a bit more sensible about the number of eggs we produce."

"Jealousy, thy name is chickadee," said the cowbird. "Now, shut your beaks!" And with that, she opened her wings and returned to the pasture fence.

"Did you hear how she insulted me?" squeaked Glynnis. "If I ever so much as see one of her eggs in anybody's nest, I will peck a hole in it." She flew up to sit beside the Yellow Warbler.

"I suppose that's one solution to the problem," Pewter dryly commented. "Murder the young."

The Yellow Warbler fumed. "First of all, the

damned cowbird isn't hatched yet, and second, the egg has no business in my nest, and last, you fat thing, cute as the baby may be, it will grow up to be as awful as its mother."

"You can kill as many cowbird eggs as you like," said the Tufted Titmouse, ruffling his feathers. He stared down at Sneaky Pie, more interested in another matter entirely. "You really think my name will be changed?"

"Mine, too?" The Black-crested Titmouse echoed the concern.

"A presidential candidate is talking about people marrying animals." Sneaky Pie relayed this with relish. "No woodpecker or titmouse is safe!"

All the birds screeched, fluttered up, then landed back on their original perches.

"We must stop the human insanity," Sneaky pronounced, warming to her subject as she looked up at the bird. They usually fled her company, but now not her prey, she held their rapt attention. "None of us wants to marry a human," said Sneaky.

"No." Again, the avian chorus.

"No, indeed!" chirped the chickadee.

"But that's only the beginning," said Sneaky. "The humans forget that we're Americans, too. We share these trees, the pastures, the rivers, and the ocean with the humans, right?"

"Yes," agreed a chorus of squawks.

"But the humans are destroying the things we need to live," continued the tiger cat. "We aren't destroying their habitat, are we?" asked Sneaky. She didn't really expect an answer. It was a rhetorical question, to try to get these bird brains thinking. Sneaky wondered for a moment why she bothered. But then, she increasingly enjoyed this public speaking. She scanned her audience.

An uneasy silence was finally interrupted by one of the iridescent Tree Swallows. "It's true. We cause them little trouble, and they cause us much. But what's to be done? They don't listen to us. They rarely think of us at all."

"Some do." Sneaky Pie admired the shining teal head and wings of the bird, its white underside in bright contrast to its swallowtail coat.

"Well, they could certainly pay us more attention," the Tufted Titmouse called.

"I propose we do something about it," said Sneaky. "I want to represent us, the *other* citizens of America." The tiger cat boldly pronounced, "They will hear our voices."

Pewter blinked, then whispered to her feline companion, "You're out of your mind."

"How can you possibly get humans to listen?" Glynnis asked, nervous as ever.

"If you think about it, Pewter and I live with one. It's a matter of psychology. While they appear to be acting like lunatics, upon study they are surprisingly predictable. We know their ways."

"You're not the only one watching them," Joe boomed, seemingly affronted. "We see them go in and out all the time, rushing this way and that, though it's true I cannot say I discern their purpose, or any sort of pattern."

The tiger nodded at the titmouse, who was smarter than Sneaky Pie had first thought. "When you live with one or two humans, you become close. They're not half bad, and they really try, or at least mine does. You train them by using a system of rewards. Works better than pecking their eyes out."

"So you actually think you can get your human to see what we need?" Glynnis was now fascinated.

"I do," answered Sneaky. "Now, it's a big step from that to becoming a presidential candidate. If enough of us band together, we might get some serious attention. Obviously, they're not that bright. It might take them a while to hear our message, but it's worth a try. Working together is the only shot we have. We must lead by example. If we can get along and unite for a cause, why can't they?"

A silence followed this. "You're right." The second of the Tree Swallows plucked out a chest feather, holding it in her beak.

Joe shrewdly negotiated, "A moratorium on cats hunting birds?"

"Well—" Pewter was about to screw the whole deal.

"I can work on that, but I promise that Pewter and I will not kill any of you."

"Let us think about it," the Black-crested Titmouse suggested, and the other birds chirped in agreement. "We have no reason to trust a cat."

"You have a reason to trust this cat." The tiger sounded convincing.

The female Tree Swallow dropped her chest feather. The white feather slowly twirled downward until it hovered right above the tiger cat. She then dropped off the branch and, with that speed and grace peculiar to all the swallows, zoomed in front of Sneaky's nose, snatching the feather right out of the air.

The other birds gasped.

Given to expressions of emotion, Glynnis shouted, "You could have been killed!"

The Tree Swallow flew back to her friend, who chided her, "That was damned foolish."

"But a good test. Besides, I can fly at a right angle if I have to."

Her friend nodded but secretly thought that no bird should ever trust a cat's reflexes, even an old one like that fatty.

"If you promise to work with me," Sneaky called up, "I will not harm a feather on any of you should you join my movement."

"We'll think it over." The Downy Woodpecker was impressed but wanted to confer with his winged companions.

A high-pitched scream overhead silenced the assembled. A large shadow played down on the cats, then a two-foot Red-shouldered Hawk alighted on a sturdy sycamore branch.

"Don't fly away," the big raptor commanded the smaller birds. "You're safe. I know some of my cousins chase after you for sport, but I don't eat birds."

"Art, where were you?" Joe, fearless as only Tufted Titmice can be, called the big fellow by his name.

"By the pond, watching the pasture," the hawk replied. "Heard all this talk over here." His dark eyes and black curved beak pointed down to the two cats. "It's one thing to make a promise to these squirts. What about hawks, falcons, goshawks, ospreys, eagles?"

"We're all Americans. We share the earth."

Sneaky's green eyes met those of the bird, who was bigger than she was. "And let me tell you something, Art. You have federal protection, but that doesn't protect the land or the waters. Just means you can't be hunted."

"*Hm-m-m.*" Art glanced around at the other birds, who were breathlessly awaiting his response.

"We need one another," Sneaky said, voice clear.

"What about the game I hunt?" Art wondered. "How can you represent both me and mice? Have you thought of that?"

"I have." Well, she hadn't really, but she'd wing it—so to speak. "If our living places, the foods we eat, are not polluted, poisoned, or plowed under for a housing development, things will balance out. I can't tell you not to hunt mice. I can only tell you to trust a natural balance. That's why there are predator and prey animals. Too many of one or the other and everyone suffers. It's yet another example of an imbalance of power."

A murmur attended this.

Art inhaled deeply, his mighty chest pushing out. "Cat, you got my vote. Good luck."

The birds chirped, Sneaky thanked the Red-shouldered Hawk, and the two cats headed back up the dirt road to the barns.

"How can you get our human to understand, much

less all humans?" asked Pewter. The gray cat thought Sneaky Pie might just be losing her mind.

"I don't know," Sneaky answered frankly. "But that doesn't mean I won't find a way. The more animals we talk to, the more ideas I'll get. I'm convinced dialogue is necessary."

"Sneaky Pie, we're old friends, but I think you're crazy."

"Maybe we have to be just a little, you know?"

As they reached the top of a small hill, from above the cowbird suddenly swooped, pooping right onto the tiger cat's back before flying away.

Pewter couldn't help but laugh. "Well, there's a vote of confidence."

Sneaky Pie laughed, too. "That cowbird is making her opinion known. I suppose it's a form of free speech. I just didn't realize politics would get so messy so fast!"

CHAPTER 3

Of Mice and Men

The human had left the television on before disappearing into the kitchen. Seating herself directly in front of the noisy machine, Tally grinned as she watched a dog driving a Subaru. It was her favorite commercial. The rambunctious Jack Russell sniffed the screen but didn't smell the car-driving dog. Madison Avenue admen were using dogs to sell cars.

"People trust a dog more than they trust a cat," Tally concluded.

"Ha. That dog is driving that car only because he'll work cheaper than a cat," pointed out Pewter, highly offended by the ad. "It's like the entire species has no pride at all."

Tally growled. "You don't know what you're

talking about. I heard all those dogs have agents. And the film crew can't overwork us any more than children. Furthermore, cats are too small to drive. You couldn't see over the dashboard."

"I can drive." Pewter was sitting on the sofa as she watched the TV, but she now jumped down to squarely face Tally. "Porsches were made for me."

"If you two start a fight, we won't get to go up to Monticello," Sneaky Pie reminded them.

"She's right," Tucker agreed. The corgi wanted to go to the big house on the hill.

"She started it." The gray cat peevishly glowered.

"I did not." Tally growled again, and everyone was reminded how excitable Jack Russells could be.

Sneaky wearied of both Pewter and Tally being so touchy.

"You said people trust dogs more than cats," Pewter grumbled.

"They do," said Tally. "Man's best friend. Fido. It's Latin or something, meaning faithful. Has a cat ever been named Fido?"

"Tally, no cat would endure it." Sneaky smiled. "Still, I agree, for some reason people trust dogs more than cats. What's your point, Tally?"

"You should turn over your campaign to me."

Tally wagged her little tail. "I'll name you my running mate."

Pewter exploded with laughter. "No one in their right mind would vote for a Jack Russell. And by the way, Tally, no one believes you speak Latin."

Although she agreed with Pewter, Tucker kept her mouth shut. Jack Russells lived for excitement. Finding none, they'd create it. Washington, D.C., didn't need any more frenzied yapping. It needed level heads making informed decisions. Tally thought with her nose, and was unfit for office.

Tally was getting worked up right now—not a formula for profitable dialogue. "They will so vote for me. Don't forget: I kill vermin. I protect humans. I, I, I chase delivery people. I mean, how do you know that delivery person isn't actually a thief? And I'm small, so I can get places other dogs can't. I am the most useful and helpful dog any human could want," Tally boasted.

"You're also stark-raving mad. Even given today's degraded standards, I don't think politics is quite ready to go to the dogs." The gray cat's eyes grew larger. "You run in circles, you run after everything that moves, you bark all the time, and I must tell you, it's the worst bark in the world. In the entire world."

"Is not," barked Tally. "Is not!"

Their human peeked in from the kitchen. "Will you shut up?"

Tally looked up at the woman. "Will you get a face-lift?"

Pewter cuffed the little dog. "Be glad she doesn't know what you're saying."

"That's my challenge," Sneaky said.

Pewter gave this some thought. Impressed by the Red-shouldered Hawk's response that afternoon, she reconsidered her former rejection of Sneaky Pie's ideas. "I think explaining to the world why you live with a Jack Russell will be a major problem."

Baring her fangs, mostly white, the tricolor dog growled. "You watch your mouth."

"Well, Tally." Sneaky Pie tried to sound reasonable. "Americans love golden retrievers, Labradors, even poodles. If I choose to select any dog as a running mate, out of political necessity I will have to pick one of the more popular breeds."

"No fair. I should be a candidate."

"Sorry, Tally," said Sneaky. "Your demographics are wrong. Jack Russells aren't that popular. And Pewter is right, you bark too much."

"Who wants a big fat Lab?" Tally shrieked.

"I agree with her there," Tucker said, coming to Tally's defense.

"Much of America wants a Lab," Sneaky rejoined. "They fall for their dumb good looks."

The gray cat thought out loud: "Poodles don't shed. You might want to think about that."

"Poodles are too French," Sneaky said. "Not American enough."

"Hey, over here!" Tally yipped. "I'm American." The Jack Russell's voice rose. "I'm as American as apple pie."

For a moment, the thought of pie caused them all to fall silent. What was their human doing in the kitchen?

"If you were born here, yes," Sneaky said to Tally. "But considered all-American? No."

The little dog was deeply shocked. "How can you say that?"

"You're associated with England, the British Isles. So is Tucker. You're also associated with horse people, and lots of Americans think those people are rich. That's not the message we want to send." The tiger cat considered what kind of dog would really be a good addition to her ticket.

"What? Horses mean wealth?" asked Pewter. "That shows you what humans know. Living with a horse is a ticket to poverty. They eat while you sleep." Still, Pewter was giving Tally the evil eye.

"We can deal with horses later," said Sneaky. "I can't ignore them, you know. Nor cattle, either."

"You're ignoring me!" Tally whined.

"I am not ignoring you. I am simply telling you how humans perceive Jack Russells."

The dog looked imploringly at the tiger cat. "Sneaky, you don't think I'm a nutcase, do you?"

"Of course not."

"How can you lie like that?" Pewter spat out, aghast. "You know she's bonkers."

"Pewter, let's consider this rationally. True, Tally is exuberant with her many feelings. She expresses them perhaps more than is wise, and loudly, but she's a good sort. And she does protect our C.O." Sneaky used their nickname for their human.

C.O. stood for Can Opener.

Tally triumphantly bumped the cat. "See?"

Given Pewter's bulk, this attempted bump knocked the little dog off balance, not the hefty cat.

Pewter stuck to her guns. "She's a lunatic."

"I'm courageous, high-spirited, good company," countered Tally. "I am the perfect running mate. We're in a depression. People need their spirits picked up."

"What they need is jobs," Sneaky reasonably replied.

"What about an older, wiser dog who works,

who demonstrates proven skill?" asked Tucker quietly. "Herding dogs? Hunting dogs? I myself herd cattle."

Both her friends stared at her, surprised. Before they could say a word, their human called.

"Let's go."

Once settled in the truck, they watched the lush scenery pass by, twilight casting long Prussian blue shadows across spring green meadows.

"Are you serious about this?" Pewter asked Sneaky. "You really think you need a dog as a running mate?" Pewter raised her nose, enjoying the higher view a truck affords.

"Sure I do. People aren't likely to be moved by a goldfish."

"I don't see how you can pick one running mate without offending every other breed," Tucker prudently observed. "I mean, what if you do pick a golden retriever or a beagle?"

"Good point. It has to be a mutt." Sneaky Pie watched a Great Blue Heron flying overhead to its nest by the water. "It's all about demographics."

"A mutt? Never." Tally yelped. "Have you no pride?"

"Tally, shut up!" the driver reprimanded.

Tally grimaced. "Can't we find her a mate? Something to occupy her?"

"Then there'd be two of them to manage." Sneaky laughed. "One is bad enough."

Pewter laughed, too.

"Maybe you're right. It's tough enough as it is protecting her. She can't even smell. Just last week she was twenty-five yards from a bobcat and didn't even know it. Luckily, bobcats aren't vicious, but what if she had been that close to something really aggressive? Or an animal with her young? I tell you, none of them have the sense to get out of harm's way. Sometimes I go to bed exhausted just from chasing off bad actors." Tally held her chin up, threw out her chest.

"Tally is right," Tucker said with feeling. "We dogs must be ever-vigilant around humans. Age is no factor. Adults are as vulnerable as children. Good eyes. Bad noses. So-so ears. Can't run worth a damn. Living with a human is a full-time responsibility."

"You all do a good job," Sneaky said soothingly.

Pewter raised an eyebrow but kept her mouth shut.

"You can't pick a mutt, really, Sneaky," Tally said, showing a touch of Virginia blood snobbery.

"You'd better never say that publicly!" the tiger warned. "This whole country is made up of mutts. You just button that thought right up."

"What are you talking about?" snapped Tally. "Humans are mutts. They're mixed up worse than a dog's breakfast."

Sneaky replied, "A mutt is a mix of blood, usually smart and strong. Anyway, most Americans like to think that when they think of themselves—you know, the old melting-pot stuff?"

"Surely they can't believe that." Tally remained unconvinced.

"Tally, Pewter, and I are mutts," said Sneaky. "I don't know my bloodlines." The tiger cat watched a house light switch on far away in the darkness of the country.

"Speak for yourself," said Pewter. "I am descended from a Bolling." Pewter momentarily got all grand, naming an early Virginia family. Robert Bolling of Chellowe was granted a charter for viniculture to grow grapes in the Colony. That was long, long ago.

Knowing better than to argue ancestry, Sneaky conceded, "A formidable family. Robert Bolling used Jefferson as a lawyer when he was right out of law school. Our C.O. was just talking about that with one of her friends."

"I also have a splash of Venable blood," Pewter bragged.

Venable, like Valentine, was a Virginia surname with some punch.

Sneaky bit her tongue because she wanted to say "So do hundreds of thousands of Americans by now." That would have started another fight, and things had been quiet in the truck.

The truck stopped at the gate to Monticello. After they were waved through and they parked, they climbed the hill to the house of the director, Leslie Bowman, and her husband, Cortland Neuhoff. Dogs, horses, and one beautiful daughter completed the picture of a tranquil existence on Jefferson's mountain.

"I'm leaving the windows open, but you all stay here. You know the drill." The C.O. closed the driver's door and walked to her meeting.

Tally hung out the window.

"Get back in here!" Sneaky hissed. "She always turns around, and then she'll come back and run the windows up within an inch of the top. We have important work to do."

The dog slunk down, crouched beneath the steering wheel. "She can't see me now."

The two cats observed intently as their human walked toward the house. "Okay, she's in."

Pewter was already halfway out the window.

"I'll open the door," said the tiger cat. "That's

easier than you dogs trying to climb out the window." Sneaky pressed on the door lever as the dogs leaned against it. It opened just enough for them to drop down to the running board. Freedom!

The tiger cat followed. "No noise," she ordered.

The four animals trotted up the hill toward Monticello, moonlight enshrouding the well-beloved house.

Hovering like an upturned half moon, the signature dome gleamed silver. Early May air carried intoxicating smells from the vegetable garden, as well as the flowers surrounding the back of the house. The roses alone sent off aromas like Eden itself. The drone of insects was subdued, the occasional owl call echoed over the abandoned house. No matter how much a national treasure it was, no house is alive without cats, dogs, people, children playing, fighting, loving—just breathing within its walls.

The four friends paused.

"Once upon a time we would have smelled the horses, the other cats, the poultry," Sneaky mused.

"Oh, the humans don't care. It's all about them," Pewter airily replied.

"And just how far would Mr. Jefferson have gotten if cats hadn't kept the rodents out of the grain, out of the pantry, and furthermore, where would he get the goose quills for his writings?" Sneaky stood, transfixed by the magical view.

"You mean a goose helped write the Declaration of Independence?" Tally was far more transfixed by the lingering odor of a rabbit, who had recently scurried to her burrow.

Sneaky walked toward the front entrance. "Well, he couldn't have done it without the quill, now, could he?"

"The door's closed." Tucker noticed the hand-blown glass in the special windows Mr. Jefferson had designed so they could also be used to go in and out of the house.

"I can see perfectly well," Sneaky snapped. "I'm trying to remember where the little hole is, so we can crawl in and come up by the window in his bed-room."

They walked to the left of the door, inspecting the ground.

"Was it here?" Tally found a small aperture in the foundation, which had been repaired.

"Damn. I hate all this improvement. Well, come on. Let's go down to the kitchen and the walkways underneath. You know they'll miss something," Tucker suggested.

Trotting down to the brick labyrinth underneath

the finely furnished rooms, the three gloried in the wonderful spring grass underfoot.

"Who goes there?" an irritated voice called out.

"Friends of Mr. Jefferson's cats," Sneaky called up to a house wren, now peering over her nest and none too happy at that.

"There are no cats here. The last house cat left with Dan and Lou Jordan." The wren cited the former director of Monticello and his wife, who'd worked miracles at the place and had been loved by all, including the house wren.

"Guess that makes your life easier," Pewter sassed.

"You couldn't catch me if your life depended on it."

"Really?" Pewter scratched the base of the wide tree. "Why don't you come a little closer?"

"There should be cats at Monticello—along with cattle, horses, whatever Mr. Jefferson had living with him. We all improved his life and the lives of every human here." Sneaky warmed to her subject. "They'd still be flying the Union Jack here if it weren't for us."

"I agree," said the wren. "For a while, the Jordans had a kitty in the big house, but there was *concern*—don't you love that word, *concern*?—that the cat might scratch a visitor."

"That's one of the reasons we're here," declared Sneaky. "Our human is at a meeting at Leslie and Court's. She loves all this history stuff, so we thought we'd come along for the ride, and here's why. If humans keep fading further and further from reality, which is to say nature, the day will come when even you will be removed from Monticello."

A pleasing warble followed this. As she had a syrinx, the house wren could make two different sounds simultaneously. "Too much catnip, kitty."

"Go ahead and make fun of me, but the day will come when someone will fund a study, some government type, to prove that your poop carries harmful genes. You and every other bird will have to be removed from Monticello, and they'll take the caterpillars, too. Some of them bite, you know, and humans just hate insect bites."

"I never thought of that."

"Start thinking," said Sneaky. "As it is an election year, folks are losing their common sense. Bird poop. I mean it."

"What about poop?" asked the wren.

"Toilets. The humans think they've solved the problem, but then they really haven't. Their poop still has to go somewhere."

The corgi's eyes shone in the moonlight.

"Treatment plants," Tally piped up.

"Have you ever gone by one of those plants?" Pewter wrinkled her nose.

"Of course not," twittered the wren. "I have better things to do with my time." She tossed her little head.

"Well, in the New World Order, you will be found guilty of littering just for doing your business naturally. Spreading germs, they'll say. And I don't think humans will invent toilets for birds," Pewter said.

A disconcerted twitter followed this. "Heaven forbid! You're scaring me. You're trying to get me to fall out of my nest."

Pewter—at the base of the tree, voice so sweet—called up, "We know better than that."

"I'm asking you to think about the rest of us taking over this country. We outnumber the humans," Sneaky encouraged the wren.

"You plan to seize power by brute force?" the wren asked, snapping her beak shut nervously.

"Absolutely not. We're nonviolent. We need to vote," Sneaky said.

"I can't vote. I can't write."

"You can hold a pencil in your claws and make an X. And we can all overrun the polls. I believe we can get this country back on track and protect ourselves. You know." Sneaky sat for a moment. "It will save them, too."

"You might have something there," the wren said breezily.

"While you think about it, and there's no big rush, I'll be back up here in a month, as Mom comes to meetings here once a month," said Sneaky.

"Do you really consider a human a mother?" The wren leaned farther over her nest, which just made Pewter tense all her muscles. There really were muscles under the lard.

"Well, the four of us call her the Can Opener, the C.O., but we love her, and she does care for us. And we don't remember our real mothers," Sneaky replied.

"That's so sad. My little chicks know who their mother is."

"Have any?"

"Not this year. My friends and I keep an eye on the food supply. Maybe next year. I love having little wrens."

"We're trying to get into the house, but the passage we knew under Mr. Jefferson's bedroom window has been filled up. Is there another way?" Sneaky asked.

"Sure. Go up through the old larder. The opening is big enough, easy."

"How do you get in?" Pewter asked, as though this was mere curiosity.

"Usually we don't. Causes such a fuss. But in good weather, if I need to, I'll go right through an open window. There's always a thread loose or something else I can use to spruce up my nest."

Sneaky headed toward the brick walkways as instructed. "Thank you."

"It's nice to think that Monticello still has some uses. A thread from a chair would be very nice." Tally liked chewing things, and silk or satin was a rare treat.

"'Tis," Tucker agreed.

In the old larder, they found the opening, a gap behind a back shelf.

"I can't see." Tally coughed as she squeezed into the space, careful not to knock over crockery. Fortunately, it was heavy.

"Stick right behind Pewter," ordered Sneaky, from outside.

"Just what I want, Tally on my rear end," Pewter complained.

"Oh, Pewter, shut up," the diminutive dog snapped back. "You can see better in the dark than I can."

"I can't fit," Tucker half boasted as she tried to squeeze in.

Sneaky took a quick look around. "Stay here and guard us."

"I'll miss all the fun," the corgi whined.

"We won't be long," Sneaky promised her.

And it wasn't long before they emerged from under the bed in Monticello's little front bedroom.

"Come on," ordered Sneaky. "We've no time to waste, gawking at old furniture."

The tiger cat hurried across the polished floors ahead of Pewter and Tally, past the Great Clock, powered by heavy cylinder-like weights descending through a hole in the floor into the cellar. The beautiful dining room had been rehabilitated, thanks to a gift from Ralph Lauren for which the famous designer asked no advertising. He just did it because he loved Monticello. Just behind this room, the small party found a wooden door, its handle just out of reach.

"Stand here and stand still," Sneaky ordered Tally before climbing on the dog's back, reaching up, and easily turning the old doorknob. "Onward," the cat ordered.

The back stairway reverberated with four beats each for the two cats and the dog. They came up to the Dome Room, empty but for gleaming moonlight streaming through the large circular windows and oculus skylight.

A walkway surrounded Jefferson's famous dome. Doors at intervals allowed workmen to get to the dome itself for repairs—fixing leaks, mostly. At the bottom of each door was an opening, just about cat size. The two cats zipped in, and Tally, a bit bigger, squeezed through.

Four busy mice stopped cold in their tracks.

The boldest shouted, "You get out of here!"

The tiger cat challenged them: "You aren't supposed to be here, either."

"We are descendants of Mr. Jefferson's mice. Who else would be here?" The big mouse took a precautionary step backward.

"Well, we are FFV, First Felines of Virginia," countered Sneaky, "so we have every right to be here. And Pewter here is descended from a Bolling who married Mr. Jefferson's daughter. If indeed you are descended from Mr. Jefferson's mice, you know perfectly well about the marriage to John Bolling, a fat fellow who drank too much. So there."

This caused a moment of confusion.

The smallest mouse piped up. "There haven't been cats up here in forever."

"That's obvious." Pewter could smell all the mice and see the little treasures they'd dropped around their mouse holes.

"So why are you here? Don't think you're about

to have any mousy treats. We're close to our escape routes; you can't catch us," the big mouse defiantly pronounced.

"I don't want to kill you," Sneaky declared.

"Speak for yourself," Pewter muttered under her breath.

Tally whispered, "Pewter, don't piss Sneaky off. We have to ride all the way back home, remember?"

"Well, what do you want?" demanded the biggest mouse.

"I want you and all the mice here to help me run for president."

"A cat for president?" The little mouse lifted up on his hind legs, putting his front paws together in delight. "You're even stupider than I thought. Who would want to be president, much less a cat? Isn't it all just a wee bit far-fetched?"

"Far-fetched, maybe, but it was far-fetched to think we could break free from England," said Sneaky, "and who would have thought that the skinny redhead who wrote the Declaration and served as Virginia's governor—working on all manner of things—would wind up president? I mean, everyone knew General Washington would be president, but, well, Jefferson had to fight for it when his time came. Just as we'll fight for it now."

"Why ever bother? Mr. Jefferson didn't much like being president." The smallest mouse uttered this with pride. "It's not even on his grave monument, which he designed."

"He said he didn't like being president." Pewter thought all that denial suspicious. "But he pressed on, didn't he?"

"Once you're in the traces, how do you cut them?" The middle mouse, also a bit fat, chimed in: "He was stuck."

"He was vain." Tally finally spoke to the mice. "Humans all think they can make such a big difference. Time washes all their so-called accomplishments away."

"Not Mr. Jefferson's work," Sneaky corrected her friend. "Think of all that he wrote. And he sent Lewis and Clark on their way. And what about the 1803 Louisiana Purchase? Then again, maybe you're right, Mr. Mouse, he couldn't kick over the traces. I might be vain, Tally might be right, but at least my vanity serves you all. We have little choice but to stop the madness."

"People, you mean, nuclear stuff—that kind of madness?" asked the little mouse. "We hear about all that, even up here." The little mouse grew sober.

"And it will creep closer and closer if we don't speak up, organize," said Sneaky. "So I am here to ask for your blessing. What could mean more than to have Mr. Jefferson's mice endorsing my campaign? And don't think people won't notice that mice are supporting a cat."

Flattered, the mice chattered in a group. Then the medium-sized mouse stepped forward to play devil's advocate. "We're safe here. Who would disturb Monticello? Who would even put out a cigarette butt on Mr. Jefferson's walkway, much less bomb the place? We have no need of politics."

"Oh, but you do," Sneaky warned. "Monticello is a symbol to the world of freedom. There are people out there who fear freedom for other people, and of course we know they care nothing for animals. Those enemies are outside our country's borders, and within, as well. People who want to control others, who want to put the bit in a human's mouth like they do a horse. Support from Monticello's mice would be wonderful, and think about this if you don't think much of me: How long before the exterminator fogs out this dome? There's more and more human regulation. All that has to happen is someone sees evidence that you live here and it's curtains!"

"Oh, no!" The little mouse wrung his front paws.

"They're losing their reason," Sneaky said, off and running in her speechifying mode.

"They think they have a greater right to this house than you do," Pewter added, fueling the fire.

"But we were born in this house!" the big mouse squeaked. "We have document fragments that our great- and great-great-great-grandparents saved from the wastebaskets. We have fragments of Mr. Jefferson's notes. Have they no shame? How dare they!"

"They can and they will if we don't stand up for our rights. We are all Americans." Sneaky was getting the hang of campaigning.

The big mouse stepped forward. "When the time is right, we will publicly support you."

After warm good-byes, the three visitors retraced their steps and met up with Tucker, promising to tell her everything later. Silently dashing under the sleeping wren's tree, they reached the truck just as people were gathered on the front steps of the director's house. Their historical meeting was over, but they couldn't stop talking. Humans everywhere seemed to love the sound of their own voices.

Sneaky, the leanest and most athletic of the animals, hunkered down, then sprang up, sailing through the window. She pushed on the door latch so Tally, Tucker, and Pewter could scramble in. It was hardest for Tucker, but she made it. They spread out on the seat, pretending to be asleep.

Their human reached the door, noticed it was ajar, and opened it to view the four animals sleeping.

"Aren't you all good kids?" She slid in, put the key in the ignition, fired up the motor.

As the truck pulled out of the drive, the two dressage horses owned by Leslie and her daughter shook their heads. They had just observed the cats and dogs making it back into the car in the nick of time.

The big bay gelding laconically said, "Just when you think you've seen everything. I wonder what Mr. Jefferson would have said. . . ."

CHAPTER 4

Cowbirds and the Trickle-Down Theory

"Never." Great Bess clamped her mouth shut, although sweet grass stuck out of it.

The lower pastures by the narrow river branch grew the best hay.

"What about you?" Sneaky Pie asked the second heifer: an old Angus.

"I'm with Great Bess." The black heifer, Addie, agreed with her Baldy friend, who was half Angus, half Herford.

Tally, a sometimes irritant to the two girls, blared, "It's because Sneaky Pie wants a mutt for a running mate, isn't it? I mean, she should choose me. Everyone loves a Jack Russell."

Great Bess lowered her big head. "I don't. You're a pain in the ass."

"Me?" The dog's warm brown eyes opened wide.

"You, you little hairy rat dog. I am sick of you chasing Addie and me."

Addie nodded. "No matter how often I kick, you slip by me and under me. And you have the nastiest bark in the world."

Sneaky, hoping to divert a bovine bitchfest, stepped closer to Addie. "I could name a Baldy or an Angus to my cabinet."

"Politics stinks." Great Bess spat out her grass. "What you want to mess with that stuff for?"

"I can make things better," the tiger cat stoutly replied.

"Bull." Addie snorted. They both laughed, as the bull had been dead for years.

"Tell me why you won't help me," said Sneaky.

"It's because you want a mutt for a running mate," Tally repeated.

"Shut up, Tally. They didn't know anything about a running mate."

Addie glowered at the rough-coated pack of dynamite. "Well, we know you sure shouldn't pick Tally. You nip at us, you run your mouth all the time, and your tone is so piercing. Awful. And worse than all that, you got no more sense than a yellow stick."

Tally wondered: Did a yellow stick have sense? This kept her quiet for a moment or two.

"And you run in circles," Great Bess added to her complaints. "Makes me dizzy. Jack Russells are living proof that humans are mental, seriously mental. They could have just stuck with cocker spaniels, you know." She winked her big eye at Addie.

Both big girls laughed uproariously, hay bits, grass blades falling out.

Tally dragged out the old complaint. "Cocker spaniels were ruined by breeders in the nineteen thirties."

"You were ruined from the get-go," said Addie. The little heifer blew stuff out her nostrils right at the dog, who dodged it.

Sneaky Pie looked at Tally, then at the bovine girls. "All I want is to know why you won't support me. The cattle industry is one of the biggest money-makers in agriculture. You could say that cattle made this nation, and if anyone argues that, you can sure say cattle made the West."

"True." Addie nodded.

Sneaky Pie had done her homework. "Last year cattle brought in about seventy-four billion dollars, and that doesn't count ancillary business— you know, the feed stores, the feed lots, the vaccines and vets. There's a lot of money made by you all and a lot of money around you. What about the barns built for you all, and special run-in sheds?

And cattle are predicted to make even more money this year. Big, big bucks."

"So they can kill us and eat us." Great Bess forcefully hit the nail on the head. "If you're president, you can't stop that. Each year between thirty-two and forty million steers and heifers are slaughtered. They eat meat and"—she reached out to nip at Tally—"so do you."

"Well, I am an obligate carnivore," Sneaky honestly replied. "If I don't eat meat, I die."

"Well, you eat more fish and chicken than cow," Addie said. "But if you become president, you can't shut down a huge industry."

"No. That's true, but I can make it more humane."

"Get those humans to eat chicken, or just carrots." Addie kept her eye on Tally, but the carrot remark made Great Bess jump in.

"She's right. Humans aren't obligate carnivores. They can exist on vegetables and wheat, stuff like that." Great Bess flicked her ear.

"That's true, too," said Sneaky, "but even if I could convince humans to change their habits, it would take years. You can't just pull the plug on something as big as the cattle market. At least if I can make this feed-lot process and the trip to the killer more humane, that's a step in the right direction."

"You two never went to market." Tally sidestepped another lunge by Addie.

"No," said Great Bess. "We live in paradise. Good pasture, lots of water, sometimes grain—plus, the human comes down to feed us apples. Oh, I love apples. We're lucky. We came to a good person when we were calves."

"Yes, but back to the central problem," said Sneaky. "This isn't a cattle farm. This is hay and timber, mostly. She would make a lot more money if she did run cattle." Sneaky considered this. "She can't take anything to be slaughtered. Just can't do it, so she struggles. Do you know how much money she could make with a herd of one hundred head of high-grade cattle? Let's say she sold fifty each year and bred back the best fifty, which she kept. At today's price, and I know this because I heard it on the ag report on the radio, cattle are bringing four dollars and forty cents a pound, give or take. She'd make about two hundred thousand dollars once you subtract the feed and the net costs, et cetera. The four-forty per pound is meat price. Doesn't count bone. But two hundred thousand dollars is really good money. So you can see why most humans run cattle."

"I can see it. I don't have to like it," Great Bess said.

"Even if reducing dependence on beef meant some cattle would live as companions to humans, herds would be drastically reduced or phased out altogether. Vegetarian ways could mean the extinction of some breeds," the cat said.

"Sneaky Pie, I'll be long gone by then, and so will you," Great Bess bellowed. "Give up this idea. Let humans steal, rape, kill one another. We can't do a thing about it."

"I think I can. They are deeply irrational. They need reasoned leadership."

"Hormones. They're brainless, really." Addie noticed the Great Blue Heron, the daddy, flying overhead. "He gets taller every year."

Great Bess looked up, too. "When he stands and stretches his neck all the way up, I bet he's six feet tall. Skinny, though. Well, herons are. Back to hormones. Addie is right. Scrambles their brains. We only have that problem about twice a year. They are demented around the clock."

Tally piped up from where she was sitting on the soft grass. "Is this what our Can Opener calls *testosterone poisoning?*"

"Rat dog, I don't think estrogen is any better." Great Bess let out a belching laugh.

"You've got a point there, Great Bess," Sneaky said. "They're just a hot mess, but they're clever. They use what brains they have to justify all their irrational behavior. Well, I've taken up a lot of your time. I appreciate you hearing me out."

"Pussycat, you are a decent sort. You've always been polite to us. Give up this crazy idea. You can't save anybody or anything, including us. Fate, you know."

"Great Bess, I aim to make my own Fate."

As the two animals walked away, Great Bess turned to Addie. "Not wise to tempt Fate, you know."

Up at the house, Pewter was tempting the C.O., who was scrambling eggs.

Tucker slept under the table.

"Come on, put one out for me," cried Pewter. "Fresh eggs are the best, like candy."

"If you put your paw on this bowl one more time I'm getting the squirt gun," the human threatened.

The squirt gun rested on the kitchen sink.

"That's low, really low. I need protein. Selfish."

The Can Opener did put the two eggshells on the counter for the cat to lick.

The back door, wide open to catch the breeze,

afforded a majestic view of the Blue Ridge Mountains. The less majestic view was of Sneaky Pie and Tally running this way and that for all they were worth while a flock of enraged cowbirds dive-bombed them from above.

"We are not no-counts," one shrieked.

"Laying an egg here and there in another nest is good policy," another squealed while executing an impressive threatening swoop.

"Cheap bastards." Tally snarled as she ran.

"You have offended every cowbird in this state, in the nation!" the original cowbird, who laid the egg in the Yellow Warbler nest, warned. She plunged toward the cat's head at a forty-five-degree angle.

The racket brought Pewter, Tucker, and the C.O. to the door.

Tally barked furiously while Pewter ran out, leapt up, grabbed a diving cowbird, and broke its neck. "Ha! Kill and eat your enemies."

The flock, however, was thick enough that Pewter didn't have a chance to even pull off one feather. The three animals bolted into the house to avoid the human, now armed with a broom.

The C.O. leaned the broom up against the door. "That was dramatic."

The human knelt next to Tally; no damage was

done, but the Jack Russell had suffered a direct poop hit. A wet rag took care of that indignity.

"Well, Tally, now I can say you are full of poop." Tucker laughed.

Tally did not.

Pewter stated the obvious to Sneaky Pie: "I don't think you can count cowbirds among your supporters."

"I didn't think there were that many on the farm." Sneaky took a deep breath.

"Oh, there aren't. She went out and sold her tale of woe," Tally replied. "She blathered on about being insulted. The cowbird insult story is probably making the rounds in Maryland and North Carolina by now. Tomorrow it will have reached even farther north and south. Cowbirds have big mouths."

"Guess so." The tiger, chastened, sat down, then smelled the eggs. "I knew you didn't come down with us for a reason. Breakfast."

"I get tired of canned food and crunchies," said Pewter. "I like what she eats."

"Pewter, you'll eat anything," said Tally. "You'll eat greens with fatback." The little dog acted superior, a joke, given her indiscriminate appetite even if a bit hungry—which was always.

"It's the fatback, soaks through all those collard greens. Yum."

The dog wrinkled her nose. "Pewter, greens are disgusting."

Sneaky observed the two eggshells on the counter. "Did you get two eggs?"

"Nah, just the shells."

"You know, if the wrong people get in the White House, eggs will be off-limits."

"Huh?" Pewter raised her eyebrows.

"Unborn chickens," the tiger cat declared.

CHAPTER 5

Back to the Land

The lightning bugs, pinpoint divas, had yet to make their seasonal debut. The cats, dogs, and human loved that first night when darting dots, ice yellow and pale green, filled the meadows. While the beguiling insects were eagerly awaited, a mid-May night offered many consolations. Twilight lingered, then night finally came, and with it that dampness peculiar to the night air, fragrances made more potent because of it.

Central Virginia's springs exceeded the expectations of even those who had lived in this area all their lives. While the area's fall could disappoint, with little color or a high wind taking away the red, gold, and orange leaves, spring lasted about two full months, with glorious colors, aromas, and giddiness. As the redbuds hit full blossom, an early-blooming dogwood might swell to a big, white bud, light green at the base of the unopened petals. And even with a tight bud, one could see a flaming azalea's promise. Daffodils, jonquils, tulips, all of them overlapping—some early, some right on time, some late—covered the earth like a holiday carpet.

Sneaky Pie and Pewter sat to the right of their human as she fiddled with the computer on her desk in the study. The sweet smell of late-blooming lilacs and early-blooming roses swept into the room.

Being rural and off the grid, the human used an nTelos air card, which worked pretty good. The cats could use the computer and didn't hesitate to do so when the C.O. turned it off or left the room. If she folded up her computer, they couldn't open it. But usually she left it open, and the clever cats could use it with ease.

With Sneaky Pie looking at the screen from the side, the C.O. was reading information from Open Source Ecology, a fascinating group that sought to lower the barriers to entering farming, building, even manufacturing. While their farm's human was born and raised among agriculture, Sneaky Pie realized most Americans were not. Indeed, the average age of a farmer in America was fifty-seven. In

Virginia it was fifty-five. Successfully escaping urban life, a dream for many downtrodden city dwellers, might be even more possible if they had the right information before leaving the concrete canyons. It would be good to get young humans farming.

On the floor the two dogs resented the cats' ability to sit next to the computer.

"What's she reading?" Tally wagged her little tail in anticipation.

"She's looking at the design for a walk-behind tractor," Sneaky called down. "Before that, she read about this group setting up headquarters in rural Missouri."

"Far away," Tee Tucker commented.

"West of the Mississippi, but the soil's good—you know how excited she gets about soil." Pewter had no fondness for digging—which the dogs did, of course.

"Better than here?" Tally inquired.

"Since a lot of what we have is red clay, yes," Sneaky replied. "Although we can make bricks with the best of them. A few days ago she was looking on this site at a design for an earth brick press. This OSE is amazing."

"She's not going to make bricks, is she?" The

corgi got fatigued by her human's endless ideas and projects.

"No. She's just curious." Pewter watched as the design came closer, a portion of it enlarged. "I like this stuff, but it's hard on the eyes."

"Harder on ours than hers. Our eyes are better, so we can see the little pulsations. They really can't, but you know these computers emit radiation?" Sneaky had her doubts about much of technology.

"Good. You'll glow in the dark." Tee Tucker chuckled.

"Shut up," Sneaky replied. "Back to clay. Right here on our farm, we have different soils. It's red clay on the higher elevations and really good soil down by the river. Well, it's a creek at this point, but miles away it becomes a river."

"Better for scent," Tally said solemnly. "I can lose rabbit scent quickly on the clay, but down by the river it holds. Chasing rabbits is very healthy, you know. If humans would do it, they'd have better wind and they wouldn't get so fat."

"Sitting on their ass for eight hours a day or more is going to make anyone fat. No way out," Pewter declared.

Tally giggled. "You should know."

"Asshole."

"Such pretty talk." Tally responded by baring her teeth.

"Imagine if our Can Opener knew what you were saying."

"If she knew what I was saying, she'd agree with me. You're trouble. You've always been trouble, and you always will be trouble. Your brain is no bigger than a gnat's."

The little dog barked. "Just wait. You just wait."

"That's enough." The human sternly stared at the dog.

"I will get you," the Jack Russell muttered.

"Yeah. Yeah." The gray cat saucily tossed her head. "Back to gnats." She reached over and pushed at Sneaky slightly. "They do no good. Didn't you say you couldn't even think about having insects be part of your campaign because they have six legs and that's two too many?"

"Yes. That, and they haven't much brain." Sneaky wondered where this was going. Pewter was trying to agitate her.

"What about earthworms? You've been talking about soil. And we'd all be much poorer without earthworms churning it, making it richer." Pewter was right, Sneaky had to admit.

"Well, true, but I can't talk to earthworms, and

we haven't anything to offer them. What's more, it's kind of about poop, isn't it?"

"Sneaky, the cattle poop in the fields, the fields are dragged, and that enriches the soil. So what's the difference with worms? They're not insects with six legs."

"Pewter, no."

"And there are billions of them! Imagine a gathering of all the world's worms."

"I'd rather not," Sneaky said and sniffed.

"Just you wait," barked Tally. "Pewts gonna get worms." She laughed her dry dog laugh.

"Look who's talking, wiggles," replied the gray cat. "If you didn't get your worm medicine, you'd be really gross. Actually, you're really gross now, Tally."

The human got up from the desk to go to the kitchen.

"Can it." Sneaky reached over to poke the mouse. "Pet food," she said under her breath.

"Yeah!" Pewter gazed at the screen rapturously. "Hey, what are you doing? I thought we were getting food."

"Trying to find how much money people spend on pet food each year, including bird food." Sneaky Pie was interested in economic policy.

"Now's our chance to order the really good stuff,

that expensive canned stuff she never springs for. She won't know, and she's left her credit card next to the computer."

"Pewter, money motivates humans. It's a serious defect. Profit is all too often their god. If I'm going to be an effective candidate, I need to prove how much economic value we have. Now, keep your paws off this mouse."

The two dogs craned their necks but couldn't see on top of the desk.

"Got it!" Sneaky Pie declared, after a Google search. She read the results aloud: "Fifteen billion dollars per year on cat food. About fifty-one billion dollars is spent per year on all kinds of pet stuff."

Tee Tucker heard approaching footsteps. "Get away from the computer."

The two cats jumped down before the C.O. returned, iced tea in hand, with a sprig of fresh mint twisted in it. Sitting down, she looked at the screen, which Sneaky had cleared.

"Dammit to hell! What did I do wrong now?"

Within a minute she was back on OSE's page.

Tally gave Pewter the evil eye. "What's she want with a walk-behind tractor?"

"Curious, I guess." Tucker shrugged.

"She may be curious. We need to be smart." The cat thought out loud. "How much money is spent each year buying new tractors, new implements, repairing old tractors, and the truly important figure: gas? If you have a walk-behind tractor, you might reduce the gas bill for the whole country."

"Hey, simple enough: Hitch up a team again." Tucker, smart as corgis are, thought how nice it would be not to hear the noise of those big-ass diesel engines, smell the nasty fumes. "Mules, horses, oxen. Worked for centuries. Will work now."

"Some perfect twit would complain about more methane gas from the poop from the horses," Pewter stated. "I mean, really, it would take thousands of animals to replace tractors, which would mean a monumental increase in poop."

Sneaky considered this. "Well, maybe someone would complain about methane, but when you have numbers that show the reduction of carbon monoxide, no more dependence on foreign oil, and less outlay of cash to farm, that ought to overcome that argument. And as we said before, the poop dries, you drag over it, and it becomes fertilizer—fertilizer without petroleum in it."

"*H-m-m.*" Tucker pondered this. "But most humans don't know how to plow with animals anymore."

"They can learn." Sneaky was adamant. "They've

done it for thousands of years, not just centuries. They can do it again."

"But what about animal abuse? Farming with animals requires years of training. It's better if humans are born to it. For example, a human really has to know horses. It's not something they can get out of a book." Tally joined in the discussion, forgetting to be angry with the gray cat.

"I expect a group like this OSE can teach people about old-time plowing, too, and in every farming community there has to be someone who remembers the old ways."

"Sneaky, you're talking about someone who is one hundred years old." Pewter looked up at her human, raptly pushing around the mouse.

"There are people who learned from their grandparents, their fathers. There are still enough vital people who know how to do it."

"What about the equipment? The collars, the traces? Only the Amish can make it now. Rigging a plow team costs about eight hundred dollars. The show harnesses cost a fortune, but we're talking about work teams." Tucker liked the sound of jingling when horses were hitched up. She'd heard it when carriage drivers competed.

"This would open up fantastic opportunities for other people to work with leather," said Sneaky.

"And those businesses also wouldn't be dependent on oil or electricity. Maybe they'd need some electricity for a sewing machine, but returning to some of the old tried-and-true methods would save a lot of energy. And you'd get to hold what you make," the tiger cat added.

"So?" Pewter didn't quite get that.

"How can you hold a computer screen? And who wants to hold a bunch of papers? If you *make* something, that's real."

"Hey, Sneaky, it may be real, but think of all the money that's traded every day, and no one holds one dollar bill." Tally wasn't as unsophisticated as she sometimes appeared.

"Problem Number One." Sneaky's pink tongue stuck out for a second. "If you can't hold it, smell it, bite it, how do you know it's real?"

"You forgot sex. Humans act like money is the same as sex, but can they have sex with it?" The Jack Russell's eyes brightened.

"Don't be vulgar." Sneaky frowned. "Did you already forget about elevating the discourse?"

"I thought you were interested in economics," Pewter countered. "Porn is probably the biggest industry in the world, but I don't get it."

"Why pay to see people carry on?" Pewter was mystified.

"It's a human thing," Tucker said. "We can only carry on when we're in heat. They're in heat all the time. No time-out to relax—yet another flaw in their species."

"It must be exhausting," Tally said. "But I'd be willing to try."

"You need to be spayed," Pewter said sharply. "You're getting mental."

"I said I will get you. Now I'll get you twice."

"I'll live in constant fear, I'm sure." The cat sniffed.

"There is no human heat cycle," Tucker said before asking, "Is that why they bred past their food supply?" Sneaky appreciated the corgi's acumen.

Tucker thought aloud. "They have no sense. They haven't a clue when it will be a good harvest or bad. They can't monitor their breeding, and they'll breed beyond the water supply, too. They can't help it."

"What a horrible thought," Sneaky whispered. "They will consume the earth. I'd never really thought about how they have no breeding time-out."

"Takes a long time for a human to be self-sufficient. Six years, I reckon," the corgi said. "But the way it is now, six years is useless. Few kids perform chores in the field. Young humans aren't allowed to work when they are nearly adult. So they're a drag on everyone, and on themselves, too. Even when they're eighteen, they have trouble. Just fifty-four percent of humans between eighteen and twenty-four have jobs now. What are the other half doing? How can they learn a trade? Just like dogs, humans need to work. I need to herd cattle. You need to catch vermin, all three of you are vermin killers. We have serious jobs. We start early in our lives."

"I have to think more about all this," Sneaky softly said to Tucker.

"You know those books she reads," the corgi said, nodding at their human. "There used to be wars and famines, big famines in China, millions starving to death. Terrible diseases. The human population was kept in check. Now, with medicines and technology and industrialized agriculture, millions upon millions survive." Tucker continued, "As to war, they will always have them, but they're little ones, strategic bombings rather than worldwide conflicts."

"That sounds awful," yipped Tally.

"Well, Tucker, I can hardly discuss any of that in my campaign," said Sneaky. "It will send humans right over the edge."

"Perhaps, but your idea about farming the old way makes sense. That would get more humans and animals working on the land. Maybe they could regain their natural balance. They'd be paid labor, but they'd be out in the fields plowing and harvesting. Instead of seeing twenty combines over a field, you'd see hundreds of people and horses. The big firms would alter their technology to save energy. It really wouldn't be slower if they hired enough people. And people need to work. When they're out of work, all sorts of terrible things happen." Tucker kept going. "If they're working outside, maybe they will respect nature more, including their own natures."

"That's a stretch," Pewter opined.

"Is it any further than this OSE thing?" Sneaky considered. "I've got a lot to think about and a lot to find out. First I need numbers, and then we have to figure out how to get more support. And then how to get even our human to see this."

"Mother's not bone stupid," Tucker replied.

"Sometimes she's darn close." Tally didn't say this maliciously. "How come you called her Mother? You hardly ever do that," the dog asked Pewter.

"She tries. She wants to be loved." The cat held up one paw, unleashed one sharp claw. "And don't think you can brownie me."

"I said I would get you. That doesn't mean I can't be curious."

"Curiosity killed the cat," Sneaky interjected

into the agreement, repeating the old saw. "Least you didn't say that."

"Dog eat dog." Pewter half laughed. "I could amend that. Cat eat dog."

"Lame," said Tally. "If you can't come up with anything better than that, shut up." The dog growled, but not loudly.

Pewter took the bait. "*Um-m-m*, dog in a manger."

"Cat got your tongue," Tally snapped back. Trading animal clichés as insults.

"Dog days," Pewter said.

"Pussyfooting."

"Sick as a dog."

"Pussy Galore," Tally shouted.

"I like that one," Pewter said with satisfaction. "That's a character in an old James Bond movie."

"Still used a cat word." The dog defended her choice.

Tucker, sleepy now, mumbled, "Imagine the English language without all the contributions of animals. Humans would be so much poorer without us, wouldn't they? Can any technological phrase— you know, like 'boot up'—carry the meaning or weight of 'bell the cat'?"

The four animals felt much the better for this discussion.

CHAPTER 6

Fish Tales

"Row, row, row your boat, gently down the stream. Merrily, merrily, merrily, merrily, life is but a dream," Tally warbled under the delusion that her singing pleased everyone.

The waters of the Rockfish River couldn't drown out canine noise, to the small animal party's dismay.

Tucker thought Tally's voice too thin and high-pitched, but as another dog it sounded semi-okay to her.

The two cats, however, moved downstream from the clamor.

"Is there no way to shut her up?" Pewter stared down into a deep, quiet pool surrounded by large rocks, the flow of the stream barely disturbing these placid waters.

Sneaky leaned over to see her reflection in the water. "Oh, let her have her fun."

The tiger cat's reflection was obliterated as a small-mouthed bass, a rockfish, hence the name of this river, leapt up, splashing her. "Gotcha!" the fish squealed in delight.

Sneaky, shaking off the freshwater, growled, "What have I done to you?"

The fish popped his head out of the water again. "Nothing. It's just that you look so funny. You're lucky I didn't bite you."

"Ha! I'd have crushed you in my jaws."

"That's what you say." The rockfish swam in lazy circles on the water's surface.

Pewter drew closer to the water herself. "Can you see underwater?"

"Naturally."

"Can you see out of the water?" Pewter's face was now close to the medium-sized fish.

"I can but not as well. I suppose it's kind of the reverse of your eyes." This fish was the gabby sort.

After wiping her face, Sneaky asked, "Do you fish know much about humans, Mr. Rockfish?"

"We know enough to stay away. We know any floating food that looks too good to be true probably is, but still some of us get snagged. There are always dumbbells who take the bait."

"Applies on the ground, too." Pewter knew all about baiting, although for most species this was illegal in Virginia.

"Well, some never learn." The fish sank down, then came back up again.

"Are there many of you in this pool?" Sneaky wondered.

"Depends on the time of day. Right now, no. I'm just here because I like this spot. It's under the shade of the sycamore and is nice and cool. Going to heat up today."

"Yes, it is," the tiger cat agreed. "A midspring warm day."

"So how do you stay cool?" The fish was becoming curious about these two cats.

"Air-conditioning," Pewter quickly said. "Our human has air-conditioning."

Sneaky laughed. "We sit under shade trees just like you swim under them."

"What's it like to be close to a human?" the fish asked. "Do they smell terrible?"

"Some do," replied Pewter, drawing even closer to the water's surface. "Oh, you just ignore them. Purr every now and then, rub against their legs. But you can't believe a word they say."

"Your human is the lady, the farmer lady?" The fish thought for a moment. "They can't help being what they are. They move so ungracefully, not like us, with our fins and tails."

"Never thought of that." Sneaky lifted her eyebrows.

"Land creatures don't. At least four feet is better than two. Two feet is ungainly, don't you agree?" The fish dove down, then came up again.

"Mr. Rockfish, you probably don't care much about human politics, but I want to run for president." Sneaky smiled. "I'm sure you have concerns about pollution in the water."

"Hell, yes. I think about the poor oysters in the Chesapeake Bay. The humans have created so much damage they have to reseed the Bay with sprats and pray they grow to be oysters. It's working, some. In 2011, Chesapeake Bay oysters just for Virginia brought in well over eight million dollars—something, but a pittance compared to the past."

"The humans are making a real effort to save the Bay," said Sneaky. "Our human reads aloud to us about this because she cares about 'Save the Bay.' She says that the 2011 oyster catch was two hundred thirty-six thousand bushels, but in the nineteen sixties sometimes it was three million bushels a year!" Sneaky informed the small-mouthed bass.

"Good for the Bay. What about rivers?" The fish continued, "Listen, pussycat, every drug a human gobbles up, for whatever reason, eventually finds its way into our waters."

"What?" This surprised Sneaky.

"Drugs. They take prescription drugs, then pee them out. I mean, have you any idea how many chemicals are in the water? Probably no one does, really, but us fish can tell you it sure is different nowadays. We know some of the plants we eat aren't flourishing, stuff like that."

Pewter said, "But they have water treatment plants."

"For humans—as if they gave a fig about us. Some of these drugs are so new, no one knows the long-term effects—not for them, certainly not for us. Not all those chemicals break down. It's like radioactivity; these humans love mixing up chemicals. Some stuff lasts a long, long time. If the hopped-up humans don't eliminate the drugs from their bodies, sometimes they just flush the pills down the toilet, you know, what they don't use. The drug has a date, they don't need it anymore or the date has passed. Whoosh, comes down to us and it's like an LSD trip," the rockfish told them. "You never know what those humans are ingesting— sometimes when it ends up in our water, it's like the sixties all over again. I'll swim to a spot and I can taste it. I figure whatever that is, it came right out of the bottle. Believe you me, I swim the other way. Sometimes it's poison. I just say no."

"I never ever thought of that." Sneaky was aghast.

"Not too many creatures have." The rockfish then said in a happier tone, "We adjust, but you never know what's just past that next bend in the river. Now that there are so many people, there's more and more pollution. Don't they taste it in the water? Are they really so ignorant?"

"Yes, I'm afraid so," said Sneaky, "but I thank you for pointing me in the right direction. I need to learn more about this, though I'm not quite sure how. The two of us"—Sneaky indicated Pewter—"sit by that lady you mentioned when she gets on the computer or reads. We learn a lot then, but she totally hogs the Internet, so much so that on this fact-finding mission I've instead decided to talk to every creature I can. I believe it's still possible to prevent humans from more and more self-destructive behavior."

"What a mouthful," said the bass. "I hope you can do it, but you'll need land creatures. Us water dwellers can't get to voting places. Even the giants, the saltwater mammals and huge fish, can't leave the ocean. Now, they would have real pull! Hu-

mans just *love* whales—not so much rockfish." He giggled, which came out as a burble.

The wind shifted, and they could again hear Tally's singing.

"Tally, turn down the volume," Sneaky shouted.

"We can hear that noise even underwater, you know." The fish burbled again. "Terrible, just terrible." Then he sent up a little spout of water, which hit Sneaky square in the face. Burbling again, he dove back under the water, the bubbles rising like pearls.

"I should have snagged him when I had the chance." Sneaky stepped back, wiped off her face.

"What an interesting fellow." Pewter watched Sneaky sit on her haunches and use both her paws simultaneously.

The two cats walked back to the dogs.

"Ready?" Finally Tucker had had enough of Tally's singing as well.

As the four walked through the meadows and back up to the barn, Tally continued to croon his tune.

"Tally, have mercy," Tucker begged at last. Even the patient corgi had limits.

The Jack Russell stopped, twitched her white mustache. "I thought you liked my singing."

Tucker was diplomatic: "Uh, perhaps less force-fully and less of it."

"Tally, you sound like a scalded dog." Pewter was less polite.

"Pewter, your nose is always out of joint." Tally half closed her eyes before lunging for the cat's tail.

The gray cat easily avoided this. "You might be fast in a straight line, half pint, but you will never have the fresh moves of a feline."

As they climbed the hill, seemingly small in spring but it could send a car sliding backward in winter, they continued to chat.

"Did you watch the news this morning?" Sneaky asked Tucker.

"I heard it. Why? I mean, I was half asleep. It seemed boring."

"I did," Tally volunteered. "I watched the news. I was waiting to see if it would rain."

"I know you saw it. You sat next to me on the chair." Sneaky did love the little dog, silly though she might be.

"So why do you want to know if Tucker saw it?" asked Tally.

"Corgis have measured judgment."

Tally didn't really know what that meant, so she said nothing. Still, she was ready to disagree, in case she was being insulted.

Pewter sniffed. "The usual song and dance. I mean, even when these old white and now black guys quit running, they don't shut up. I expect when more women run for office they'll blab all day, too. They never shut up." Pewter herself could go on and on at times.

"Well, what struck me was what these men do to their wives and families." Sneaky felt the sun on her fur. It felt good. "They sacrifice their offspring to their careers."

"Doesn't matter if it's political or corporate life, does it?" Pewter flicked her tail to the left, as Tally was on her right. "Humans have screwy priorities."

"I think it's worse in politics because the wives have to pretend to agree with their husbands and the children have to shut up." Sneaky called up memories of First Ladies past.

"Those women have to know what they're getting into," Tally sensibly answered.

"I'm not sure anyone really knows how bad it is," Sneaky replied. "But you are right. The wife is an adult. It's the children I feel sorry for. And when they're in the spotlight at that gawky stage, it must be painful for them."

"Humans do go through an ugly phase." Tucker laughed. "We don't, ever notice?"

"The horses do," Tally blurted out.

"Tally, shut up. What if they hear you?" Sneaky reprimanded the dog, for horses grazed nearby in various pastures.

Jones, the thirty-five-year-old Thoroughbred, lifted his head, mouth full of grass, then returned to grazing. That Jack Russell's voice could cut glass. The old fellow was a friend to all.

"Well, they do," Tally whispered. "Some horses look every bit as bad as some humans in their teens."

"Be careful," said Sneaky. "We wouldn't want to damage anyone's self-esteem. Self-consciousness never did anyone any good," the tiger wisely added. "But what got me thinking about this is that Bible-thumper who thinks people will marry animals. There's a whole segment of that strange thinking in one political party, not that the other party doesn't have some strange ideas, but at least they don't focus on sex."

"Sex with animals!" Tally screamed, and ran in circles.

"Tally, you need to be spayed. Honest to God." Pewter wanted to knock the dog sideways.

"Calm down, Tally, calm down." Tucker, who could best pacify the canine, did just that. "No one is going to sleep with you."

"I would die. I would absolutely, positively die." The little dog rolled her eyes, the whites showing.

"Folks like him always swear they are running for your children's future and their children's future. If you're doing it for children, why are they ignoring the masses of human children living in poverty? The numbers are disgraceful and shocking." Sneaky's voice was clear.

"They're all hypocrites," declared Pewter, the realist, some might say cynic. The fat gray cat moved closer to Sneaky.

"You're right," said Sneaky. "They all lie. They say they care about their marriage, their children, but it's all about them. Egotism. They imagine they have a higher calling than being a husband and a father. Selfish. Can you believe how deluded they are?"

"Yes!" barked Tally quickly. "And my voice is the only one amongst us that counts, since all three of you are spayed. So the solution to this kind of abandonment of family is to neuter the humans who want to run for public office."

"Excellent idea!" Sneaky agreed. "It will focus the men and calm the women. You are so right, Tally. I will definitely add that to my campaign platform: Spay or neuter your pols."

CHAPTER 7

Training Humans

Opened on the kitchen table, *The Wall Street Journal* caught the eye of both Sneaky and Pewter, both of whom had jumped on the kitchen table as soon as their human walked outside.

The forbidden ever entices.

"Hey." Pewter clawed a newspaper photograph of a dog's paw, bigger than her own.

The photograph covered nearly one quarter of the page.

"National Disaster Search Dog Foundation," Sneaky read out loud. "What a good ad. Pewter, think of how many humans search-and-rescue dogs have saved in the last few years."

"Well, the ad says it takes ten thousand dollars to

train one dog. Do you think humans have at least enough good sense to give to the foundation?"

"Let's hope so." The tiger cat sat on the effective ad.

Pewter's brilliant green eyes opened wide. "It's in people's self-interest to take care of the animals trained to help them. There are Seeing Eye dogs, dogs that hear for people, dogs that save people from attack. Dogs do a lot of work, I've got to admit. Of course, cats have saved people, too. Remember Homer, that cat who saved his human from an intruder standing right at the foot of her bed? And Homer's not the only one. We cats fend off animals lots bigger than we are. I personally can be ferocious."

"You're scaring me," Sneaky cracked.

"But back to this National Disaster Search Dog Foundation. And, of course, cats are superior. It's just the two of us, I can speak frankly. For one thing, dogs can barely read. But you must give it to them, Pewter: They do these jobs better than we could."

"It's the digging. Tally and Tucker can ruin Mom's garden in a heartbeat. Dogs can dig through rubble, and the big ones can pull people to safety. It is impressive." She then lowered herself closer to the tabletop. "Did those two twits hear me?"

"No, they're asleep."

"Whew. There'd be no living with them." Pewter exhaled.

"There's no living with them now."

They both laughed.

"They brag that their noses are so much better than ours. If their noses are so great, why are they always smelling the most disgusting things? We have good noses. I can smell anything that Tally and Tucker can smell—not that I'd want to." Pewter put her paw on the ad paw, and it fit just inside the photo paw.

"Well, are their noses better, or do they smell scent faster?" asked Sneaky. "Think about how quickly foxes react. Can they smell us before we smell them?"

"No. Foxes really throw off, maybe even control, their odor, that odor, like a sweet skunk." Pewter thought about this. "No, I don't think foxes' senses are better than ours or the domesticated dogs', either."

"Then why are they always ahead of us, and particularly ahead of the Can Opener?" Sneaky had watched her human try to take photographs of foxes time and time again. The foxes would invariably duck into their dens or just motor on.

"Maybe they do pick up scent before the rest of

us. Foxes are uncanny." Pewter respected the beautiful creatures.

"I better talk to them." Sneaky put her paw on top of Pewter's.

"This photo, you can see the trimmed claws." She removed her paw so Sneaky could put her own inside the photo.

"Be easier if dogs had retractable claws like us. But since dogs don't climb trees, they don't need them. Then again, gray foxes climb trees, and they don't have retractable nails."

"Neither does C.O., and she can climb trees," Pewter noted. "I wonder why she doesn't climb trees more. Why don't humans climb trees more?"

Sneaky ignored the question. "I'm thinking of those nail colors, remember? The time she painted her nails purple? Painted her toes, too. Why would any living creature want purple nails and toes?" Sneaky wrinkled her nose. "So strange."

"Maybe she's color-blind."

"Wouldn't we know?" Sneaky stood up.

"How would we know?"

"Perhaps you're right, then," said Sneaky. "She must be color-blind. Purple nails." The tiger cat listened to the snoring of the two dogs. "Those two swear they don't snore."

"Everyone who snores does that. It's odd." Pewter returned her attention to the ad. Those rescue dogs were genuine heroes. "Can you imagine how exhausting it would be to try to search for suffering people? Or animals? You can smell fear."

"Yes, you can, but I bet what they really get a nose full of is blood." The tiger pondered this. "Suffering cuts across all species. Remember when our colt had a heart attack, dropped, and thrashed around? Two years old and such conformation. Dead in five minutes. You never know."

"Never forget that. Here today. Gone tomorrow." Pewter half smiled.

"Pewter."

"Well, we all have to go sometime. Might as well accept it and live life, and do whatever you want to do. No point dwelling on bad news. Now, see, that's what I really don't understand. The TV, the radio in the truck, the Internet—all that jabbering, and most of it bad news. X shot Y. A building collapses in Cairo. Hundreds of cows freeze to death in Europe. A terrible storm sends a big wave that wipes out everything in its path."

"That was an earthquake under the ocean," Sneaky corrected her.

"Doesn't matter. It was a total disaster by anyone's definition."

Sneaky sighed before getting up. "I suppose there's

nothing we can do about stuff like that, but there's still something we can do about laws, the way people treat us, and the way they treat one another."

Pewter started to disagree, then she too rose on all four feet. "I am less concerned about that than about what Tally will do to get even."

"She's already forgotten it." Sneaky jumped on a painted kitchen chair and then to the old wooden floor. "She has the attention span of a three-year-old child."

"Hope you're right," Pewter said under her breath as they tiptoed past the two dogs snoring on their sides.

"Ever notice how different dog personalities are, depending on breed?"

"Sneaky, why ever would I waste my precious time thinking about dogs?" Pewter affected a grand air.

"Because you live with two of them."

"I live with grasshoppers, too, but I don't dwell on them. Dogs do what they're told, eat, sleep, chase things, and try to hump everything."

"Unneutered males. You're being unfair."

Pewter, sashaying along, did not immediately reply, then: "Okay, they're better than grasshoppers, but really, they are a lower life-form."

"That's what some humans think about us."

"Well, why should I care what any human thinks?

How much credibility do they have? No matter how cranky, no cat ever started a world war."

"No cat lives outside its nature. They do," Sneaky said.

"What's that got to do with killing millions and millions of people, to say nothing of the cats, dogs, horses, birds, you name it, that get in the way of the humans' guns? Mother quotes statistics about how many people were killed in this war and that war, but she never quotes how many people starved or died of disease, and not once has she given figures for the animals, and how they suffered and died." Pewter warmed to her subject.

"She did tell us that one and a half million horses and mules died in the War Between the States." Sneaky offered a mild defense.

"I suppose that's a start. Look, you and I know that dogs have owners, cats have staff. Our dear Can Opener may not know she's staff, but she performs all those functions." Pewter laughed as she headed straight for the Can Opener, sitting at her desk.

Sneaky laughed, then she, too, walked into the office, books piled in stacks on the floor, on shelves, papers also stacked neatly.

"Some of these books are really old." Pewter

stopped to inhale. "You can smell the dust. The paper is different from current paper, you know."

"She's got enough of them." Sneaky leapt onto the desk, where one pile of papers had the human's full attention.

Pewter also hopped up. Outside the window, low clouds made the night even darker, as not one star could peep through.

"It's not healthy to work at night," Pewter announced, then grabbed the pencil right out of her hand.

"Hey!"

"You will ruin your eyes." Pewter's green eyes looked directly into deep brown ones.

"Come on, Pewter. I need my pencil."

Taking the pencil back, the human started scribbling anew.

"You really ought to listen. Your eyes are meant for daylight. Artificial lighting isn't good for your eyes. You should clean up and go to bed. If you leave these papers, I'll take care of them."

"Pewter, you'll push them all on the floor." Sneaky now sat on the left side of the person.

"Exactly. Paperwork makes her mental." The gray cat grabbed the pencil again.

"Cat."

"Flatface." Pewter pulled harder at the pencil.

The C.O. noted the time, 9:30 P.M., on the old mantel clock. "It's too late. I can't think anymore."

"Go to bed." Sneaky chimed in with Pewter.

So the human put down the pencil, stood up, cut the lights, and left the room.

"You just have to know how to train them." Pewter whacked the pencil so it skidded off the desk.

CHAPTER 8

A Hoot

A night chorus of peepers, bullfrogs, and Whippoor-wills serenaded a soft spring night. The nocturnal Chuck-will's-widow also sang out in its throaty "chuck."

Sneaky Pie, out for a solitary prowl, sat at the opened door to the stable and listened to the night music. Until recently Chuck-will's-widows were found farther south, but the weather had changed enough so that birds and some mammals not commonly seen before 2000 now traveled to Virginia. Last summer, Sneaky saw a Green Kingfisher down by the pond. The Belted Kingfishers lived there, too, their eggs safe at the back of a tunnel in the pond bank. Sneaky liked kingfishers, as she liked the raptors, probably because, like herself, they were meat eaters and therefore hunters.

Muskrats lived in the pond, and beavers built a lodge farther down the Rockfish River. Sneaky admired how hard beavers worked, but she didn't much like them. The muskrats, on the other hand, proved good company.

The damp night air filled her nostrils with scent. Scent intensified at night.

She often wondered about each species' gifts. What would it be like to possess the power and speed of a horse, the grace of a deer, the soaring ability of the eagle a mile up? What would it be like to be a tiny mouse gathering bits of wool, paper, and cotton to make a cozy nest? Sneaky wasn't much for nests, but she admired the skill it took to build one, especially a big one, high up in a tree. Even squirrels' nests, sloppy by a cat's standards, took effort.

Sitting there thinking about how many animals—potential supporters in her campaign—lived just in Virginia, not to mention the entire fifty states, the cat felt overwhelmed by her mission.

Maybe Tally was right. Maybe Sneaky Pie should hand off her noble quest to man's so-called Best Friend. But then she considered how ready most dogs were to appease authority. A leader needed to know when to compromise and when to fight, both intellectually and physically. A physical fight enlivened Sneaky; it focused her. You won or lost. The mouth battles never felt finished. Even if humans recognized how much Sneaky Pie had to offer them—in wisdom and experience—she couldn't imagine herself on a podium just going "blab blab blab." She didn't think those other candidates believed half of what they said, but when there were so many different types of people to woo, maybe the primary skill of a politician is being a convincing liar. The ability to effectively simulate sincerity might be the most important quality for a politician. She knew she couldn't fake it. She wasn't as indiscreet as Tally or as puffed up as Pewter. Sneaky called it as she saw it. An honest cat. Every time she thought of Pewter claiming to be descended from Bolling blood and therefore Pocahontas, she had to laugh. Poor Princess Poke. Married a good man, was carried to a strange land, died young.

Obviously Pewter was not going to die young, despite her genetics. Pewter crested ten and fudged about her age. Why, Sneaky had no idea. She herself was a mature cat, fourteen by her count, beyond the wildness of youth, although she could still chase a butterfly.

There was a rustle overhead; then the light click of claws grasping a beam caused her to lift her head to see.

"Any luck?" she called to the barn owl, who hooted back.

"Good hunting tonight. Usually is at the edge of a front. Everybody's out getting food before the rains, although the rains are far off." The owl fluffed her feathers, then smoothed them down. "Heard you're causing a lot of talk."

"I guess."

"It's an interesting quest you've embarked upon, a difficult one. But I fear our time may have passed."

"What do you mean?" Sneaky climbed up the ladder, walked across the hayloft, stopped by the beam over the center aisle, where the owl perched.

"I'm thinking of the gods and goddesses. When people worshipped them, they also worshipped us because each god and goddess had an animal sacred to them. We were sacred to Athena. Hounds and deer attended Artemis. Every god or goddess had an animal friend. But now all that is gone: We've lost our mythological importance."

"Well, the bald eagle is the symbol of the United States."

"And I am tired of hearing about it," hooted the owl. "Those two eagles on the Rockfish River are conceited beyond belief. What do they do? Sit in trees and catch fish. There's no reason *they* should be the symbol of this country."

"Perhaps." Sneaky, naturally, thought a cat much better suited to the role. She imagined her face on a dollar bill.

"Now, if the humans had more sensibly selected an owl as their national symbol, they would be blessed by wisdom. But no, they chose a fish killer." The barn owl let out a hoot of derision.

"It is strange," said Sneaky. "France has a rooster, England a bulldog, Russia a bear. So those people around the globe at least pay some attention to animals."

"Oh, pussycat, they haven't a clue. Although I do think the cock for France is just about perfect." He chortled.

"Lions, leopards, tigers, wolves, boars—even pelicans were used on shields." Sneaky liked the books on medieval life that her C.O. read incessantly.

"That was all a long time ago," said the owl sorrowfully. "No, they have forgotten what they owe us, the courage and guidance we once gave them."

"That's why I am mounting my campaign: to restore good sense and dignity across all species."

"I admire your grit. Don't know much about your sense," the owl said.

Sneaky took no offense. "We all know the Declaration of Independence. Even foxes know that."

"Yes."

" 'We hold these truths to be self-evident, that all men are created equal, that they are endowed by their Creator with certain unalienable Rights, that among these are Life, Liberty and the Pursuit of Happiness.' "

The owl, in his sonorous voice, recited, " 'That to secure these rights, Governments are instituted among Men, deriving their just powers from the consent of the governed—That whenever any Form of Government becomes destructive of these ends, it is the Right of the People to alter or to abolish it, and to institute new Government—' "

The two fell silent for a moment, then the tiger cat said, "The Declaration applies to us, too."

"Oh, it's about *people,* always *people*—and for that matter, it was only about white men." The owl half closed his golden eyes for a moment.

"You're right. As amazing as Mr. Jefferson was, he was a creature of his time. Just as we are creatures of our time." Sneaky never failed to defend the long-dead redhead.

"True."

"Were he with us today, he would see things a bit differently."

"For one thing, Mr. Jefferson wouldn't write the Declaration of Independence, he'd text it." The owl laughed loudly.

"Oh, dear." The cat grimaced. "Here's what I think: He owned slaves, he owned animals, he liked cats—but I will set that aside for now. He sort of liked women, and he sort of didn't. I mean, he loved his wife, lied about his mistress, both here and in Europe, but he thought women were lesser creatures. He didn't believe they should vote or participate in public life."

The owl blinked. "There are still people who own slaves in the world today and parts of the world where women are chattel."

"It's horrible, but the mistreatment of us is horrible, too." The cat drew closer to the beam. "If Mr. Jefferson really were alive today, I'm quite sure he would consider women, African Americans, and animals differently."

"I should hope to holler." The owl used the old Southern expression.

"So we must continue his work for him. Take his noble ideas into the twenty-first century. This country is not ruled by the consent of the governed. Heretofore, we animals have had no voice."

This oration so moved the owl that he turned his

head nearly upside down, then back up again. "You're right!"

"We need a voice!" said Sneaky. "I speak for those who haven't been heard from."

"Sneaky." The owl called the cat by her Christian name. "I admire your passion. I think you are right, but I don't know how you can expect to reach people. They all live in bubbles. For some, it's a rich bubble of consumerism; for others, it's a miserable bubble of poverty and pain."

"I know. I can't say I've entirely worked out my outreach strategy yet. Another problem is that I don't have any money. The Republican candidates have already blown millions, and the president will squander millions upon millions to get reelected. The estimates on what the campaign eventually will cost are over one billion dollars."

The owl blinked again. "Oh, my, shocking."

"The president spends as much time raising money for his reelection as he does on the huge difficulties facing our country. Everyone accepts it, says that's just the way the system works." Sneaky thought the whole process wasteful—destructive, even.

"If I were the president I'd spend less time fund-raising and more time keeping an eye on those beautiful daughters." The owl opened his eyes wide. "Those two are becoming women and they will upset applecarts. Men will lose their reason around them."

"Shows they're still animals." Sneaky laughed and the owl hooted, too.

CHAPTER 9

Cast Off Your Chains!

"Don't you just love shiny things?" Pewter held up in her paw a golden chain with a medallion hanging on it.

"Not much," the corgi confessed.

The gray cat swung the chain a bit, then dropped it on the worn wooden floor to hear the pleasing metallic clink.

The sound awakened Sneaky Pie, asleep on a kitchen chair.

Tally, under the chair, also woke up. The Jack Russell got up and stretched. Even stretched out, she wasn't very long. "Let me see," she said. "I want to see the shiny thing."

Pewter swung the chain toward the Jack Russell, who grabbed it in her teeth.

"Tastes, um—" The dog dropped the chain. "Not edible."

"You knew that." Pewter picked up the glittering chain.

"Had to be sure." The little dog sat down on the kitchen floor.

Sneaky, off the chair now, hooked a claw through the other end of the chain.

The two cats pulled, the chain's medallion sliding first in one direction and then the other.

"Fun." Pewter's pupils expanded.

"*Whoo.*" Sneaky lifted up her end of the chain so the medallion slid down to Pewter, who then reversed the procedure.

The cats, enraptured by their game, paid no attention to the screened door opening and the light footfall.

"I wondered where that was." The C.O. stepped into the kitchen, grabbed the chain.

"You weren't wearing it." Pewter tugged, not releasing her end.

"Pewter." The C.O. put the cat's paw between her forefinger and thumb with one hand while extricating the chain with the other.

As the chain swung in her right hand, Sneaky took a whack at it.

The C.O. laughed. "That's what I get for leaving jewelry on the counter."

She hooked the chain around her neck. The two cats longingly stared at the treasure.

"That necklace would look better on me than her," Pewter said, diplomacy cast aside.

"The gold would show up nicely against your gray fur," Sneaky agreed.

"I've seen dogs with heavy chain collars. I don't want one." Tally's mind turned back to the kibble in her dish.

"You'd fall down with a heavy chain around your neck." Pewter tormented the dog by going over and sitting next to Tally's food bowl.

This way the cat could pat Tally's head when the dog ate. Drove the dog crazy.

Snapping a dish towel off the rack, the C.O. polished the medallion. "Maybe I should get little steel Saint Hubert's medals and attach them to your collar. This is my Saint Hubert's medal, you know. Mother gave it to me."

The C.O.'s mother had died decades ago yet was missed every day.

"Doesn't look bad on you, it just would look better on me. Steel? No. I should wear gold." Pewter gabbled away.

"I'm not wearing a collar or a necklace," Sneaky Pie said. "I will not be put in chains."

"I don't have a choice. Have to wear my collar and my rabies tag." Tucker thought a medal might be pretty. "The tag always pulls off, so she has to keep paperwork. As if I'm going to bite anybody."

"I am." Pewter smiled broadly. "I think I'll start with you."

Menacingly, she circled Tucker, who ignored her.

Tally padded over to the ceramic bowl. Pewter charged over to the bowl.

Tally, a tidbit dropping from her jaws, warned, "You don't like dog food. Leave me alone."

"If I'm hungry enough I'll eat your food, but mine is better. Has more fat in it."

"I know," Tally sarcastically replied, at which the cat cracked her right over the skull. "Ouch!"

"Peon," Pewter snapped.

Tally lunged for her, but the gray cat easily evaded the dog by jumping straight up. She then came down behind Tally, biting the dog's tail just enough to register.

"Stop it." Tally twirled around as Pewter leapt onto the counter, looking down with a wide, satisfied grin.

"This is going to be one of those days." The C.O. crossed her arms over her chest. "Bubba pushed a gate off the hinges. Had to tie it up until I can get someone to help me. And my mortgage is due. I hate sitting down to write checks." She did, however, sit at the table for a moment.

"Sorry." Sneaky Pie jumped on her lap. "At least your necklace isn't ruined."

She looked down at the stag's head with the cross between its mighty antlers. "Mother bought this in Vienna, at a jewelry store by the Spanish riding school where the Lipizzaners are. I cherish this."

"I still think medals for the dogs is a good idea." The cat placed her paw on the C.O.'s hand, which held her medal up so she could see the beautiful work on the medallion.

Petting Sneaky's glossy head with the other hand, the C.O. said, "I love Saint Hubert. Guess Pewter does, too." She looked over at the cat, who struck a pose. "He's the patron saint of hunting and hounds. No one knows exactly when he was born, but probably around 656 A.D. He died in 727. So he lived to be seventy-one, a good age in any century, but really marvelous back then."

"Hounds? Really, is there a patron saint of cats?" Pewter looked down at Tally, winking at the dog, which only further infuriated her.

"Saint Francis," Sneaky replied. "Everyone loves Saint Francis."

"He doesn't count," said Pewts. "I mean, he loved everybody, you know. There are paintings of him with birds and all that. No, I want a saint who dedicated her or his life to cats."

"You might have to wait for that," Tucker drowsily called up to the cat.

"Well, what's the big deal about Saint Hubert?" Pewter sniffed.

"No big deal," said Sneaky. "Just that the C.O. loves the necklace and medal. But I think the story goes that Saint Hubert was a rich youth who passed up Good Friday's service in church to hunt. There weren't many churches then, as much of Belgium and Europe was still pagan. He heard church bells but paid no attention. A giant stag walked in front of him, the cross appearing in his antlers."

"How do you know that?" Pewter became mildly interested.

"Because she's told the story so many times."

"Well, I don't remember it." Pewter crouched lower on the counter, threatening to jump onto Tally.

" 'Course not," Tally shot back. "You're too busy thinking about yourself."

With that, the cat arced off the countertop smack onto the little dog. Pewter growled ferociously, pulled some white fur out, then disengaged and ran for all she was worth out the animals' door, out the screened door (which also had an animal door), and all the way to the barn.

Tally was in hot pursuit.

"Dear God." The C.O. got up and hurried outside, making it to the barn in time to see the cat scramble up the ladder affixed to the wall while the dog barked below.

"All right. All right. Enough. Come on, Tally."

The dog obeyed, angrily looking back to see the cat giggling at her.

"I'll get you," Tally growled.

"That's what you say," Pewter sassed.

Back in the kitchen, the dog drank some water while the human knocked back a Co-Cola. Then they both sat down for a minute. Sneaky had calmly watched the whole dog and cat drama unfold, as had Tucker. They sat together on the floor.

Tucker asked, "Do you really think Hubert saw a vision?"

"Maybe," Sneaky answered. "People sometimes can see beyond the veil. I don't know, but she loves to tell the story. Why not believe it?"

"You're right," Tucker agreed. "Maybe there are special days and times when we should all dedicate ourselves to doing the same thing. For them it's a holiday or church. I think all dogs should celebrate Rin Tin Tin's birthday, and Lassie's as well."

"I, for one, celebrate every day," Sneaky said and purred.

Tally dripped water on the floor off her mustache. "Pewter's funny, wanting a saint dedicated just to cats."

"You let her get under your skin. Ignore her," Sneaky counseled.

The C.O. got up, pulled out some treats for the cat and the dog, giving them out as she reminisced with them, "You all never met my mother. She was social, I mean really social, smart, and a wonderful dancer. We'd go places, and men would line up to dance with Mom. But we didn't have much money, and she always wanted to go to Austria. She loved music, and she wanted to attend the opera at the big opera house there. She wanted to see the Spanish Riding School, too. She saved and saved. I chipped in, a few of her friends did, too, and for her seventieth birthday, off she went. Pretty fabulous, isn't it?"

"It is. A dream come true." Sneaky Pie had seen photographs of the C.O.'s mother, a stylish woman.

"How old is she?" Pewter looked at their human.

"How would I know?" Tucker said.

"You know a lot else." Sneaky shifted her weight.

"But it's usually easy to tell how old they are. Especially if they're from Nordic countries. Skin can't take this Virginia sun."

"Hers is okay." Sneaky jumped back up on the table. "Well, she never talks about her age, because I think she doesn't care."

"Oh, please," said Tucker. "They all care. They're obsessed with it. Billions are spent annually by humans thinking they can make themselves look younger."

"Billions?" Tally wondered.

"Of dollars."

"Billions of dollars to look pretty, and it's not just women. Men, too. There's plastic surgery, thousands of creams and potions. Stuff they have shot into their skin, even their lips. The mere thought of it makes me cringe. Needles." Tucker closed his eyes tight.

"*Eeww.*" Tally did, too.

"Yeah, but our age doesn't show so quickly." Sneaky struggled to understand the human viewpoint. "Everyone looks good in fur."

"Needles in lips." Tally's voice rose to a high screech, making the C.O. look at her.

Tucker perked up her ears. "It does sound pretty awful."

"She's not doing any of it." Sneaky peered closely at the C.O.'s face.

"So how old do you think she is?" Tucker wondered, too.

"Hard to tell. No fat. Strong body. Moves fine. But there are deep creases by her mouth, wrinkles around her eyes, and her hair has gray in it. I don't know. I mean, she has to be kind of old, but she's not creaky yet."

"Baffles me. The whole aging thing," Tucker said. "I guess when I can't herd the horses or chickens anymore, I'll know I'm old."

"They move around more than we do," said Sneaky. "They meet more of their own species than we do. She just told us about her mother flying to Vienna when she was seventy. So maybe they want to look really good for all the new people, and young people are pretty."

"Nah, it's about money." Tucker threw out a dash of cynicism. "The young buy more junk than older people. That's why so many ads are pitched to them. They don't know enough about real quality yet, plus they need to establish households. It's all about spending. I guess that makes older people want to look young, too. You all see the stuff on TV, you want it."

"I guess." Sneaky peered more closely at her

C.O., who reached out and stroked the cat under her chin. "But I think the surest way to look old is to try to look young."

Just then Pewter, triumphant, returned. "*Ta-da.*"

Tally wagged her tail, taking a step toward the gray cat.

"You two: Cut it out." The human spoke forcefully.

Pewter joined Sneaky on the table. "Why didn't you tell me you talked to the owl last night?"

"I didn't tell you because you were too busy with the chain. I like him. He's not so much like other birds."

"*M-m-m.* He woke up when I was in the hayloft, told me some of what you all talked about. Makes me think. I mean, about gods, goddesses, and now saints. Do you think there were once giants and stuff like that? Dragons?"

"Well, in Genesis there's a mention of giants. I like it when she reads her books out loud, so yes, why not? Aren't we all evolving? Some species live. Some die off. If there were dinosaurs, why not giants, dragons, or angels?" Sneaky thought it made sense. "I think of Shetland ponies bred in upper latitudes. Maybe they lived, but fairies and giants didn't. The creatures that survived lived in the middle latitudes. You know, medium-sized things."

"You could say in your campaign that you're descended from a saber-toothed tiger," Pewter suggested.

"Cool." Tally liked the image.

"I suppose ultimately I am, but that ancestor stuff doesn't work these days. Candidates have to pretend to be one of the people, and the truth is, if you're running for president, you aren't."

"*H-m-m*. Never thought of that." Now that Sneaky pointed this out, Tucker could see it. "A candidate is supposed to be like Joe Average. Being rich is a sin, right?"

"Being rich is a miracle," Pewter replied.

They laughed. "Well, if money is the issue, then Sneaky, you're one of the people. We don't have but so much money." Tucker smiled.

"I know. And that's what I think will make our human old," Sneaky said. "She's like so many humans, worrying about money."

"Really?" Tally quizzically replied.

"Yes. She struggles. She works too long and too late, and you know what, millions of them do just the same to make ends meet. I don't want our mother to make herself old, to die of a heart attack or something just to pay the bills, the taxes."

"Millions?" Tally was aghast.

"Tally, there are seven million people out of work,

and that figure only counts those on unemployment. Who knows the true figure—those that are now off the benefit rolls, those that are too defeated and poor to look for a job? It takes money to look for a job, Tally. You need nice clothes, you need gas money and a car that will run. You need a haircut and money for parking, too. If you farm like our mom, you need constant equipment repair, and diesel fuel is so much more expensive than regular gas. Seed prices shot up, fertilizer is through the roof. You've seen her fertilize, overseed, harvest, then store her hay. That takes time, money, and help. No one can farm all by themselves. People are scared, you all, scared, exhausted, and deep-down angry."

"They made this mess," Pewter rightfully observed.

"Not all of them." Tucker was thinking along with Sneaky. "Our human never stole money from anybody. She never sold a bad bale of hay pretending it was good. Those people losing their homes were lured into it, sold a bill of goods, you know. Many, most of them, weren't financially educated. Maybe they should have known better, but they didn't. They were deceived by those crooks on Wall Street and in Congress who opened the door for the Big Boys."

"Then there's the problems with pensions, entitlements, that sort of thing." Sneaky nodded. "Both ends against the middle. And our human is stuck in the middle, along with millions of other Americans—humans and animals."

"Well." Pewter paused a long time. "I don't want our C.O. to wear herself out, to lose what she's worked for. You do see things differently, Sneaky. You provide an alternative view, and that is sorely needed."

Tucker added, "We love our human. We might not talk about it, but we love her, and she loves us. Remember when she was looking at the American Pet Products Association stuff on the computer, Sneaky?"

"Yeah, I called down the numbers to you."

"And I remember: Sixty-two-point-one percent of U.S. households have an animal in them. That's millions upon millions of dogs, cats, birds, horses, and I guess goldfish and stuff, but mostly us. All those cats, dogs, and horses love their humans. Okay. Maybe a small percentage of humans are cruel and mistreat their animals. Hell, they mistreat their children, but most don't. Those dogs and cats and such are your constituency."

"Tucker, I hope you're right," Sneaky replied.

"What about the undomesticated animals?" Pewter wondered.

"I'd like their support, too, at least some of them. But I think Tucker's right. Humans will first respond to the animals closest to them, the ones they trust. They have a hard enough time understanding us. It will be really hard for them to understand a mountain lion or a sparrow. We need to reach our own first."

Sneaky rubbed against the C.O.'s face. "So how can I tell her we want justice for all?"

CHAPTER 10

Choose Your Allies Wisely

"Don't you ever get bored?" Sneaky Pie asked the beautiful visiting German shepherd as they sauntered along the Rockfish River.

"No," the dog replied. "I like being retired."

Walking alongside the shepherd Daisy, Tucker inquired, "Why did you enlist?"

"I didn't. I'm part of a program of special breeding. We're bred for stamina and intelligence. This has been going on for a couple of decades. I don't really know, but I know the human breeders study constantly."

"Like Thoroughbred breeders or hounds, kind of like that?" Tally wondered.

"Yes. They observe other shepherds, they study bloodlines on the computers, they go to special training school. There's a lot to it, but I never had a choice. I made the grade, and that was that." Daisy stopped to drink out of the clear-running Rockfish River.

Pewter watched tiny bubbles come up, as they were near the pool. "If you go over to that pool, you'll get a surprise."

"Don't listen to her," Tally quickly intervened.

The shepherd, though, curious, padded over to the more quiet water, deep, looked down.

Up popped the small-mouthed bass. "You're a big one!" she exclaimed.

"You're a jerk," Pewter snapped at the fish before Daisy could respond.

A stream of water aimed at Pewter missed its mark as the fat cat was just far enough away. "Lucky. Come closer."

"Nope."

Sneaky again pondered thoughts of representing fish, but it got too complicated. Plus, who would want to represent this twerp?

A long stream shot from the river, this time just grazing the gray cat's chest.

"Ha, ha." With that, the fish sank back into the deeper water.

"Fish are strange," the big dog observed, before

glancing over at Tally, running around in circles. She thought Jack Russells were pretty odd, too.

The five animals trotted past the road that turned up to the barns, following instead the wide footpath along the river. The dried-mud path, cool underfoot, crossed a little feeder creek, a culvert underneath, and opened onto a lovely low meadow, the soil rich. The alfalfa and orchard grass swayed in the slight breeze.

"Two more weeks and this will be ready to cut." Tucker loved haying.

"The smell is the best." Sneaky liked it, too.

"It's a funny thing," said the visiting dog. "You'd think there wouldn't be much to smell in the desert, but there is."

"Really?" Tally always wanted to know more about a good scent.

"At first you have to adjust to the heat. You think a Virginia summer is hot, nothing." The beautiful shepherd continued, "If you drink a lot of water it helps, and my Army buddy put electrolytes in the water for me. Well, I digress. You can smell gasoline miles away, and when I worked in bomb detection, that was easy to smell, too. The humans assume it's the inside of the bomb, the actual explosive material, but you can smell the wiring; the metal really gives off an odor in the desert. A lot of times that's what I smelled first, the wires, and even though the bombs are hidden or buried, the heat works on the metal."

"Were you scared?" Sneaky liked this gentle dog.

"I was scared when they took me away from my mother, brothers, and sisters. I liked the training once I got used to being in the Army. The more I learned, the more I liked it, and there were other dogs. I didn't have to be completely alone with the humans," Daisy answered.

"Lots of humans?" Tucker wondered.

"Yeah, but they're in a special unit. They take tests just like we do and the service winnows the wheat from the chaff. The ones that have the ability to work with animals go through training. So you aren't dealing with an idiot."

"Did you work with one human?" Pewter couldn't imagine taking orders.

"Lance Corporal Kenny Falkenstein. Big blue eyes, big fellow. I loved him."

"Is he dead?"

"No. We worked together in Iraq for a year; then we came back here to train other humans and dogs. Kenny got promoted, and I was considered over the hill. The top brass wouldn't let him keep me. He tried everything. So I was mustered out, and a group of ex-service people in northern Virginia found a home for me. Most of them had worked in the K-9 units. I miss Kenny. Don't get me wrong, I like the person I'm with, I like living on a farm, but I miss Kenny. Together, we went through a lot. He emails Tiff, my new human. So I know what's going on with him."

Tiff was a lady in her late thirties, who liked competing in the agility trials. She and the C.O. were friends.

"Once you get used to a human, it's difficult to adjust to a new one," Tally said. "I don't know how I'd do without our C.O."

"Oh, one human is pretty much like another," Pewter airily rejoined, as she walked in front of the others.

Sneaky whispered to the shepherd, "She loves our human. She likes to show off; you know the type."

Whirling around, Pewter, tail up, accused: "You're talking about me. I know it."

"What makes you think I'm talking about you?" Sneaky shot back.

"Because I'm fascinating."

"Let's hang back." Tucker, low voice, warned Tally, "She's in one of her moods."

At that moment, Pewter, having taken a few steps backward, turned around and stepped on a

flat rock. A large copperhead sunning herself on the rock felt the weight, curled up, and opened her fearsome fangs near Pewter's astonished face. Pewter simultaneously jumped up and sideways just as the copperhead struck. The snake missed, saw the other animals, and with astonishing speed slid through the alfalfa straight for the river.

"She tried to kill me! I could have been poisoned," Pewter bellowed, puffed up, looking like a giant bottle brush. "How do I know she's not a small python? Was it? She came up from the Everglades. I could have been strangled."

Sneaky ran up to her. "It's okay. She's slithered away."

"I could be dead!" the cat wailed.

"Take more than one bite to kill that fat thing." Tally enjoyed Pewter's fright. "Take all twenty-two feet of a mature python to wrap around the blubber."

"I will kill you." Pewter, still quite enlarged, flew straight for Tally, who had the good sense to run.

"Are they always like this?" Daisy asked, as she watched the two zigzag, circle, screaming, barking all the way.

"Yes," the tiger cat forthrightly answered.

"The two cats at our house can be divas, but I

don't think I've ever seen a cat like Pewter," the shepherd said.

Sneaky and Tucker laughed and said in unison, "Lucky you."

Turning up to climb through the meadows and then pastures to the barns, they spotted in the distance Pewter chasing Tally on the farm road now.

Jones and his two blind pasture mates, Blue Sky and Shamus, the pony, heard the commotion. Jones, with his one good eye, described the action. All three equines snorted air out of their nostrils, laughing at the description of the fat cat chasing the little dog.

"Moves pretty good for a large cat," the shepherd observed.

"That she does." Tucker wondered how long this fight would last and wasn't looking forward to hearing about it from both parties. Tempest in a teapot. She feared it would go on for days.

Sneaky returned to life in the service. "When you were retired, did you get retirement pay?"

"No."

"Did you have a rank in the Army?"

"No."

"So you did all that work for free? No pay, no hazard pay, no retirement pay?"

"Not one penny. I did get free medical care in the service, though, but not now, of course. We rely on private citizens to help us after our duty is over."

"If I am elected I promise that all animals who have served in the Armed Forces will get pay, get retirement pay, and all the benefits that accrue to humans. I will work unceasingly for this."

"We've been in all the wars," said Daisy. "Many of us were killed. Before mechanized warfare, think of the horses and mules, and what about carrier pigeons?" The shepherd knew she and the other animals throughout time often got a raw deal.

"And yet animals are proud to serve," said Sneaky. "There were one-point-five million horses and mules who lost their lives in the War Between the States, and of all the horses taken over to Belgium and France for World War I, none came home, I think." Sneaky knew most all of them died, shoved in unmarked graves, if buried at all. World War I was unremitting horror for humans and animals.

"Would you serve again?" Tucker wanted to know.

"I would. I liked the Army, but remember I was bred for this. I think it's the same for people. Some can take the discipline and danger, but most can't. I do think we should receive compensation, though.

I mean, I can't enlist, but once any of us are in there, we deserve consideration."

"I see. What about the dolphins? The Navy trains them, doesn't it?" Sneaky wondered.

"I've heard that, but I've never met one. It's hard enough to meet land animals from the other branches of the service. Just about impossible to meet the water mammals."

"Sneaky, that's farther down the road. Stick with land animals," Tucker advised.

"She's right." The shepherd noticed that Pewter had finally collapsed under a huge pin oak.

Tally was nowhere in sight.

"Will you help me in my campaign?" Sneaky asked the shepherd. "Will you ask your comrades to support me?"

"I will," the shepherd vowed, glad to have another important task.

Once up at the barns, they joined the two humans sitting in the shade in two directors' chairs under the sloping barn roofline.

Pewter had now also joined them, but no Tally.

Leaping up when the dog and cat appeared, Pewter shouted, "No reptiles! No reptiles in your campaign! I will leave, I swear it. No snakes allowed."

Sneaky laughed. "Turtles aren't so bad, they're amphibians," she protested.

"They can snap," said Pewter. "If it's cold-blooded, the hell with it."

"There's a lot of cold-blooded humans out there," the shepherd coolly said.

"Don't represent them, either." Pewter remained adamant.

"Fine. No reptiles." Sneaky sighed, but she was just as glad not to have to talk to them. Reptiles were difficult to converse with; those split tongues of snakes always upset her.

Tally crept out of the barn.

"Speaking of reptiles." Pewter puffed up again.

"What is all this hissing and spitting?" the C.O. admonished Pewter.

"Oh, you have no idea. No idea at all," Pewter replied, with the perfect blend of indignation and anger.

Sitting right by the C.O., Tally took no chances and stayed quiet.

Sneaky counseled Pewter, "Just forget it."

"Forget it. Forget it! I could be lying down there on that rock, in the throes of death by poison or strangulation. Painful, protracted death. And she"— Pewter glared right at Tally—"makes light of it."

The woman called Tiff said, "People think animals don't have feelings, friends, preferences. Obviously your gray cat does."

"She is a creature of many opinions." The C.O. laughed, and all the animals except Pewter laughed also.

"I do have many opinions, and they are all correct." Pewter had the last word.

CHAPTER 11

Clever as a Fox

Little rain made the ground hard and the grasses brittle, tufts of the latter flying behind Sneaky Pie's paws as she raced at top speed over the back pasture toward an ancient walnut tree.

Flying overhead, the Yellow Warbler sang out, "They're gaining!"

Led by the head female, running in broad daylight, five coyotes thought they had an easy lunch.

The tiger cat summoned up one last burst of speed and made it to the walnut. She leapt high, grabbed a low branch, and scurried out of reach. She was breathing hard as she sought to memorize her pursuers' faces.

On her hind paws, the lead coyote stretched up

the tree as far as she could, but the cat was well out of reach.

"You were lucky today, pipsqueak," the sixty-pound coyote said, baring her impressive fangs.

Sneaky, with the Yellow Warbler on the branch above her, remained silent.

The son of the lead coyote, weighing about forty pounds, whined, "Momma, let's go. I'm hungry. We can bust out some rabbits."

The mother licked his handsome face, then turned and trotted off, the others following her.

"Close call," said the warbler. The pretty little bird watched the coyotes retreat.

"I never thought they'd show themselves in daylight," said Sneaky. "I've smelled them. I'm pretty sure I know where the den is. They're two miles from home."

"And my, aren't they big? Lots bigger than out West," the bird noted. "That gang of hooligans has been bragging to their relatives about how much there is to eat in the East, about how thick their coats are, and how big they are. They even boast about how they can take on wolves if they have to."

"I heard the humans say the Wildlife Department has released wolves down in southwestern Virginia. Don't know if it's true, but they're worried. Sooner or later those wolves will reach us."

"Won't be a ground nester left, or a rabbit," the bird said and sighed. The sunlight caught her feathers, so she glowed almost a neon yellow. "Why'd the humans do that? Release vicious wolves into their habitat?"

"Because wolves were once native to Virginia. Elk, too. Hey, once upon a time dinosaurs were native to Virginia. Are they next?" The cat's wind was restored, and she was back to speechifying.

The two shared a laugh before spotting a gray fox, low to the ground, speeding across the high pasture.

"Hey, come up here," the Yellow Warbler called.

The beautiful animal hurried to the walnut tree, saw the cat but came on up anyway, as grays can climb.

The gray fox settled on a lower, wide branch below Sneaky. "Smelled the coyotes," he said. "They will kill and eat anything. I believe if times get hard enough they would surround and kill a human."

"Pray for rain, because if we don't get some, times will be hard," the Yellow Warbler replied.

"We've had low-pressure systems, some sprinkles, but just not enough moisture," the fox said, nodding. "It's May, though, and rains will come. I don't worry about drought until July."

"*U-m-m*" was all the cat replied.

The Yellow Warbler flew away, then flew back. "The coyotes are heading south. Right toward all that corn partway up out of the ground."

"They'll eat some, and so will I when it's ready." The gray fox smiled. "The only thing I love more than corn, grapes. Oh, my." He smiled broadly. "And with all these wineries around here, I can't wait for those tiny bits of heaven to appear on the vine."

"I thought you liked mice and rabbits best," Sneaky said.

"Meat's always good, but I have to work for it. Unlike you." He chuckled. "If I can pull a ripe ear off the stalk or grab a bunch of grapes, easy peasy. So sweet. When I eat lots of corn, my coat shines. I'm only stating a fact. I'm rather a handsome fellow, if I do say so myself."

The Yellow Warbler twittered, "You are. What's your name?"

"Cyril. Mother gave us names starting with a C, since her name is Christina."

"Like foxhounds." Sneaky mentioned the practice among hound breeders.

"Exactly."

"How many coyotes have moved into the area?" Sneaky wondered.

"Those five," said Cyril, "and there's another pack

up on Ennis Mountain and, of course, the Blue Ridge is full of them."

Ennis Mountain was a mass pushed up by a glacier, standing alone in front of the Blue Ridge. Ridges and ravines fanned off the lone hunk of rock and trees. Once east of Ennis Mountain, no mountains cropped up. If one drove northeast, in thirty-five to forty miles, the Southwest Range loomed. Once east of that, the land rolled, then flattened, finally meeting the Atlantic Ocean.

"Ennis Mountain," said Sneaky. "I rarely go there, but sometimes Tally chases a deer up there." Sneaky thought about the Jack Russell's determination after picking up a deer's scent.

"You'd best warn her about the coyotes," Cyril advised.

"I will. Don't know what good it will do, but I will." Sneaky looked up to the Yellow Warbler. "I didn't smell the coyote until I reached Jim and Joan Klemic's bridge. When did you first see them?" Sneaky asked the fox, mentioning the neighbors' bridge, so well built that one could drive tanks over it.

"The coyotes smelled you before you smelled them," replied the gray. "But I think the cowbirds might have told them, too. They've been shadowing you."

The tiger cat considered this. "Once they're against you they're really against you, aren't they?"

"They never forget a slight." The Yellow Warbler held out her wings to catch the sun. "They won't try to kill me, but I can guarantee for as long as I live there will be a cowbird egg in my nest."

"Push it out. I like eggs." Cyril smiled.

"Believe me, I will," said the bird. "What do you think of the coyotes?"

"As long as there's enough to eat, I'm okay," said the gray. "So's the red fox. If the food gets tight, they will either kill us or run us out of the territory. They'll kill house dogs, cats, you name it. Of course, if you all travel in packs you have a better chance of fighting them off. Basically cowards, they'll avoid a fight unless they're sure they can win. They are clever and omnivorous, but then so am I, and I think we foxes are smarter than they are."

"Really?" Sneaky liked this fellow.

"I can turn scent on and off; they can't," Cyril bragged a bit.

"My human says that about foxes, and people who don't live in the country don't believe her."

"Your human puts out salt licks for the horses and cattle; I should thank her." Cyril stretched out on the broad limb. "How come she doesn't have a mate? I don't, but I'm only a year old. I will have one next year. I'll be big enough and strong enough so I can fight off my rivals. Life is better with a vixen at one's side."

"Well, I agree," Sneaky replied. "I don't have a mate, but I've been spayed. I do have three best friends, although there are days when I could kill Pewter."

"The fat gray cat?" Cyril asked.

"Yes."

"See her a lot when I'm down at the barn. She rummages in the empty feed bags before they're gathered and tied up. She'll eat anything, won't she?"

Sneaky laughed. "She likes sweet feed as much as the horses or you, I guess." She paused then said, "Humans don't always go in twos. Maybe it isn't natural for them, or maybe it once was and now it isn't."

"That's impossible," squeaked the bird. The Yellow Warbler folded her wings. "Who can you snuggle up to in the nest when it snows? A girl's got to lay eggs, and it takes two to feed them. Now, I'm not saying my mate is perfect, but he works hard and he's good at repairing our nest."

"You just wait, next year I will win the prettiest vixen in this country," Cyril dreamed.

"What about Charlie?" Sneaky asked the fox. "I

assume the gray male I see is your brother. Mother calls him Charlie."

"*M-m-m.*" Cyril frowned. "I will just have to compete for my vixen against my brother. He's cocky, but I'll outfox him. He's going to paint himself in a corner."

"He taunts the hounds, I've seen him," the little bird filled in the cat. "His brother does, he goes down to the kennels. Walks all around and taunts the foxhounds."

"They won't get him," Cyril declared. "He can evade them easily. Plus, he knows when his scent is strong and when it isn't. Charlie gets the whole hunting game. We worry more that someday Charlie will sass one of those coyotes or do something similarly reckless. If he gets killed, it's going to be the coyote or a car—I hope neither, but sometimes Charlie has no sense."

"*Ah.*" Sneaky did understand. "Well, my money's on you finding a beautiful girl."

Cyril beamed. "We'll sing together."

Foxes bark, answering one another back and forth. This is what Cyril liked to think of as singing.

"My human sings." Sneaky pondered this. "Back to this mate stuff. Humans can't find each other as easily as we do. They make it entirely too complicated. My human doesn't even look."

"Sad." The Yellow Warbler couldn't imagine life without her fellow.

"I agree. I see her sitting at the desk, doing her sums, trying to figure things out, and I think it would be easier if there were two of them doing sums, chores, planning. But who knows?"

"They drink. Your human gets a mate who drinks and it's all over." Cyril spoke with authority. "I visit most of the farms around here. I check the garbage first, of course, and some cans are so full of bottles they can't hardly put the lid on. I hear those folks fighting."

"Cyril, you are an observant fellow. Is there anything you would like humans to do differently?"

"Yes. Not drive so fast. Leave us alone. Fortunately, they're easy to fool. I can be walking behind one and they never know, even if there's a group of them. Now, if dogs are with them, that's different. Humans are so wrapped up in whatever they're talking about they miss everything around them. I suspect it's a sad life."

"Me, too," the Yellow Warbler pronounced.

"For some of them, 'tis," said Sneaky. "For others, they only need other humans. They're dead to the world around them." Sneaky reached down her paw just above Cyril's lush coat. "I want to run for president. I want all of us—humans, animals—to cooperate and live in harmony."

"*Ah*," Cyril simply responded.

"But you will never live in harmony with cowbirds and coyotes," the Yellow Warbler predicted.

"You're right," said Sneaky. "They can form their own party. But we can do something to help other animals. I can't force anyone to join me."

Cyril sat up. "Animals aren't going to live in harmony, pussycat. We eat one another."

"I know that," replied the tiger cat. "But if we trust the natural balance, I think that will work out. It's when things get out of kilter—for instance"— she looked up at the Yellow Warbler—"humans have made laws so that a farmer or a hunter can't shoot a raptor. Now, I like raptors. I understand them. We're both hunters. That's why it's easy for you and I to understand each other." She now looked down at Cyril. "But the raptors have proliferated. They have just about wiped out the woodcocks, the grouse, so many ground nesters, including the rabbits. There's nothing to stop them. At one time, things were in balance. Now humans have knocked it out of balance."

"Yes, yes, that's true," the Yellow Warbler said.

"It will take years—decades, even—to restore order," the cat thought out loud.

"Well, what about bringing wolves and elk back?" asked the fox.

"Cyril, before agriculture took over, yes, wolves, elk—who knows what else?—roamed this state. But while the mountains, the oceans, and the rivers remain, the surface of the land has changed. Once corn, wheat, barley, and then soybeans were put in, well, you can't take that land and make it wild again. I mean, unless the humans just walk off and give up farming. Cattle, sheep, goats, all those animals came here once the big predators were driven off or killed."

"True. True." The little bird enjoyed the philosophical discussion. How far back to nature could you go?

"I believe the humans have forgotten how hard their ancestors struggled and, worse, how dangerous a big predator can be. I mean, I'm a cat, but I have no desire to sit down with my cousin the mountain lion, or even a bobcat."

"The Wildlife Department says there aren't really mountain lions in Virginia. The big cats that folks have spotted are descended from big cats people kept as pets that got away." Cyril had heard the gossip. "Black panthers, swamp panthers, it's so unrealistic I can't believe anyone's gullible enough to believe that the big cats they see are or were pets. There are mountain lions in Virginia," said the fox. "Why deny it?"

"If they admit it, the government will think it has to do something about it. Don't fret the humans with the truth." When the Yellow Warbler laughed, it came out like a musical scale.

"Perhaps not," said Sneaky, "but I can concentrate on human housing development. It doesn't have to wreck the environment so much. I can focus on farming with regard to wildlife, reconsidering some of the chemicals that are used and balancing that against crop yields. Humans need money. Thankfully, we don't. But we can help make them money, a point I intend to make clear to them."

"I make humans money?" The Yellow Warbler was surprised.

"Yes, you do," said Sneaky. "People pay to watch birds. They pay to learn how to watch birds, and they go on nature walks. They stay in motels and bed-and-breakfasts. Birdwatching is a big deal." Sneaky smiled at the yellow bird, so elusive to the human eye. "That's for starters. People pay to fox-hunt—or chase, I should say. Cyril, you boost the economy, too. Think of the horse sales, the feed, the shoeing, the trucks to pull trailers, the clothes, and I haven't even gotten to the costs of the hounds. Animals make money wherever we go. If we can return to a partial natural balance—we might not get the whole way there—I believe we can make them even more money."

Cyril was intrigued. "What a thought."

"Speak to the foxes," said Sneaky. "Help me spread my message. Join my cause."

"I will. Right now, let's help each other. How about if we go to your barn? I'll duck out before the house dogs smell me. But if we travel together, that's some protection."

"Good plan," Sneaky said, beginning to back down the walnut tree.

"I'll fly reconnaissance," said the warbler. "I have to fly that way anyway, as my nest's down near the river, along with Debbie and Glynnis's nest. They are both such chatterboxes." The Yellow Warbler liked her neighbors but wondered what they said about her behind her back.

The three animals moseyed along until the weather vane of the barn hove into sight, the nose of the horse on the vane pointing north, which was a bit unusual. Winds usually came from the north or northwest, not up from the south.

They paused for a moment to view the vane.

"Verdigris," Sneaky said. "That's what the C.O.

calls it. I think she should climb up there and shine it."

"Copper has a distinct scent," said Cyril. "So different from steel or iron. It's so pretty, but it will turn green again," the gray fox predicted. "Well, I'm glad we got to talk."

"Me, too," both Sneaky and the bird replied.

As the cat headed for the barn, she felt for the first time that she truly could make a difference. And in the distance they heard the peculiar bark Cyril called singing.

CHAPTER 12

Horse Sense

At the barn, Sneaky Pie jumped up and sat on the outside bench. A soft breeze rolled up from the Blue Ridge Mountains; the paddocks and larger pastures shone emerald green; the sky, robin's-egg blue, was filled with creamy cumulus clouds. Lifting her head, the tiger cat sniffed the first tang of rain on the way. The southern wind would bring moisture from the Gulf of Mexico, far away.

Apart from sprawling on the C.O.'s bed, the barn was Sneaky's favorite place to hang out. The smell of horses, cleaned tack, sawdust, hay, bales of rich, rich alfalfa and sweet feed created an enticing stew of aromas. A twenty-five-pound bag of dry molasses rested in the feed room. Her human liked to soak up some molasses with beet pulp, which the horses loved. The human's feeding potions for her animals occupied her more than her own food, to which her body bore testament.

The cat loved to stroll down to the barn in the morning while her human scooped out food and tossed out hay and alfalfa. When the C.O. plunged her hands into the beet pulp, which had soaked overnight, a rush of molasses scent would sweep through the air.

Now that the weather proved cooperative, the horses stayed outside in the pasture most of the time. Often a horse would plop down and fall asleep on its side, looking disturbingly dead, while the other horses continued munching on the pasture grass.

However, if anything disruptive or disturbing appeared, the alert horses nuzzled the sleeping one awake, and they'd investigate or run off.

A special paddock held Blue Sky, the blind Saddlebred; Shamus, the pony, also blind; and Jones, born in 1976, one good eye. Since their routine never varied, the blind animals could get around just fine, even walking into the barn from outside if need be without much help. Being a Thoroughbred, one-eyed Jones still considered himself superior to all the other types of horses on earth. As most horses on the farm were Thoroughbreds or

Thoroughbred crosses, he would also fall back on his advanced age for superiority claims.

With a sagging back and gray face, the rest of him was still a rich dark bay. He ate, lifted his head, observed the younger horses in adjoining large pastures.

"Ozzie, one of these days he's going to nail you," Jones warned sternly.

The ex-steeplechaser, Ozzie, liked to taunt a young gelding, who had been sent from the racetrack. The very flashy youngster put up with it because Ozzie was his senior. But the steeplechaser's taunts, and his racing around in circles, were most definitely wearing thin.

"Dixieland, ha, he could never catch me," Ozzie boasted.

Dixie, as he was called, snorted, threw up his head. "You say, old man. You're seventeen years old. I'm faster than you are."

"Twerp, you were retired from the track because you were slow. I was retired from steeplechasing because I won a lot of money in a lot of special races. The man who raced me thought it was for the best. If I'm on the move, you can't touch me."

That did it. Dixie lunged for Ozzie, a 16.2H bay, whereas Dixie was nudging 15.3H and could twist and turn fast like a Porsche. Horses are measured in hands, a hand being four inches. So Ozzie was taller than Dixie. A surprised Ozzie barely got out of the young horse's way. Twirling, turning, Ozzie thundered down to the pond, flying at about a thirty-degree decline, with Dixie tearing after him. Sneaky moved from his perch to Blue Sky's special paddock. Next to Jones, mouths agape, the two animals watched what was turning into one hell of a horse race.

The blind Saddlebred, Blue Sky, chuckled. "Dixie's not a wimp."

The little pony, Shamus, listened to the hoof-beats. He could recognize horses by each one's distinctive rhythm just as he could recognize vehicles by the sound of their tire treads. "Ozzie's winning," Shamus declared.

Jones watched. "Yeah, but he had a head start."

"You're slowing down, old man," Dixie shouted, as Ozzie pulled ahead.

Two lengths behind, Dixie reached as far as he could with his neck. Baring his teeth, he made a great show of anger.

Knowing the younger horse was gaining, Ozzie headed straight for the three-board fence, jumping up and over with ease. For him, it was a piece of cake, nothing compared to the fences he'd taken in his glory days.

Dixie was still being taught how to properly jump but didn't flinch. He soared over that fence in high style.

As they neared the house, Tucker, Tally, and Pewter raced out from inside and onto the back porch, then onto the little patio. The dogs knew better than to chase the horses; plus, the horses were rolling at great speeds.

Hearing all the ruckus, the C.O. also ran out.

"Uh-oh." Ozzie turned wide, ran straight back, and jumped the fence into the pasture.

Dixie, intent on Ozzie, flew by him in the opposite direction. Halting for a moment, the youngster looked up to behold an unhappy human moving in his direction.

He, too, turned on his haunches, one quick twirl, ran back, and jumped the fence at the same place where he'd jumped out.

Ozzie, head down, grazing, didn't even look up at Dixie's entrance.

Dixie was no dummy. He also began grazing as though nothing at all had happened.

The running C.O. had reached the fence. She climbed over without much grace. "What the hell are you all doing?"

Ozzie raised his head and looked at her with his sweetest expression. "Nothing."

"Dixie!" The C.O. walked right up to Dixie, who raised his head for a scratch.

The bright chestnut appeared surprised. "Who, me?"

"What are you two doing?" the human demanded.

Ozzie returned to the serious business of eating. "Enjoying a fine spring day."

"You all better behave or I'll herd you in circles," Tucker barked from the patio.

Both horses acted as though it were just another spring day. La-di-da, this grass tastes fine.

The C.O. threw up her hands as she walked back to the house. "If I live to be one thousand years old, I will never understand what gets into them!"

Tally trotted along, her little tail straight up. "Mental, they're mental." The little girl enjoyed adopting this superior attitude, ignoring her own frequent outbursts of emotion.

"Well, you should know," Pewter snapped, unable to resist. She'd hopped up on the fence post to see what would happen when the C.O. reached the horses.

"Smartmouth." Tally glowered.

Back in the pasture, the two horses exhaled loudly.

Dixie turned to Ozzie. "You still got it, Gramps."

"Damn right I do." The bay smiled.

"They stopped," Blue Sky said, back in the paddock. "Did she scare them?"

"No, they shined her on." Jones laughed.

Shamus sidled up next to the old horse. "Back in the day, Ozzie did win a lot of money. Hundreds of thousands."

Jones snorted. "Now, now, squirt, Ozzie gilds the lily."

"He did win," said Sneaky. "I think one year he won about a hundred thousand." The cat then quickly added, so as not to contradict her elder, "But it's true he overstates his case."

"Every day. Every single day." Jones sighed. "Still, Ozzie's good about knowing his worth and what we horses generate. After all, just last year we generated one hundred two billion dollars for the economy. Of course, that's with the multiplier effect. If it's just horses, not feed stores, blacksmiths, it's thirty-nine billion dollars, but, hey, that's a lot of money for a species that people predicted would die out with the advent of the motorcar. Horseless carriages? What a mistake!"

The tiger cat nodded. "Well, they seem to still have use for you, even today."

"Ozzie told me that eighty percent of horse owners have an annual income of less than seventy-five thousand dollars, and about half of those make less than fifty thousand dollars," said Shamus. "So you know this is really about love." The old horse turned his blind eyes to the south, for the scent of moisture had intensified. "Gonna rain tonight."

"Thank the Lord," Blue Sky bellowed.

"Actually, Jones, I came into your paddock to tell you I was chased by coyotes in broad daylight," said Sneaky. "If it wasn't for the Yellow Warbler and Cyril, the fox, I'd still be up in the tree. They let me know when things were safe."

"Oh, those coyotes are trouble," said Jones, walking over to the water trough. "The only predator that kills them is humans, and the coyotes easily evade them. You shouldn't go out in the woods or pastures far from the barns alone."

"I came back with Cyril," said Sneaky.

"Yes, he's a good fellow. Usually you don't get on with foxes."

"We hunt the same game, but there's enough for everyone," Sneaky replied.

Jones laughed. "Cyril comes in the barn every night and eats what we've dropped. He's tried to get into the feed room to open the molasses bag. Foxes have that sweet tooth, you know. But I'll say it again: Cyril's a good fellow."

"That he is. When they start fox-hunting in the

fall, I'll get him a fixture card." Sneaky mentioned the card with the times, dates, and places for hunting: insider info especially useful to foxes.

"Oh, he can outrun anybody, and you know they don't kill, but I do think that would be a nice gesture."

"Jones, why do you think you've lived so long?" Sneaky asked.

"I've had the best of care. Still have my teeth, still get a bit of exercise. I think that's it, plus I do have good bloodlines." A hint of pride came into his voice.

"Mother says you go back to the great mare, Golden Apple." Sneaky knew this would please the old fellow. "And that goes back to the Tetrarch." She mentioned a famous stallion from England. "But most of all, she brags about Domino. You have Domino blood, from 1891."

"I do. One of the greatest. Stamina, brains, speed. Well, I did not have the career that Domino did, but, you know, Sneaky Pie, I didn't enjoy the track. I don't want to run around in circles, even though they're big circles. Some horses love it. Me, hated it. Once the C.O. found me down in South Carolina, brought me up here, well, everything changed. I was outside. I learned to fox-hunt so I could run over meadows, splash across streams, soar over fences, and be with other horses. Jolly fun. I need to be in the wild, kind of, you know."

"I know exactly what you mean." Sneaky did, too. "Well, I think I'll go up to the house."

"Stop by those two loonies, will you? Tell them in my day I would have smoked them!" Jones's eye brightened.

"Indeed I will."

The cat loped across the paddock, ran under the fence, and came out onto the pasture where Ozzie and Dixie grazed.

She delivered Jones's message.

Ozzie stopped eating. "Well, he would have given us a run for the money. Old as he is, look at his conformation."

Dixie paused, stared toward the old fellow. "I can see that."

"Jones also told me, Ozzie, that you keep up with equine developments, especially those involving profit," said Sneaky. She was becoming quite the economic expert, at least when it came to animals.

"I do," answered the retired steeplechaser, very pleased to talk about one of his favorite subjects. "You see, pussycat, anything that creates money is valuable to humans. That which is valuable lives. Therein lies the problem. A racehorse, a steeplechaser, loses value when we are injured, become a step slow. We used to head straight to the slaughterhouse, a horrible fate but better than abandonment or starvation."

"The worst," Dixie chimed in. "I come from Lane's End Farm in Lexington, Kentucky, and they do everything right there. Horses are treated with respect. I'm here because, really, I wasn't meant for the track. I'm kind of like Jones that way. He tells me he didn't like to run, and I didn't either—not at all—but I like what I'm doing now. I even like the exercises over the tiny little jumps, cavallettis, and the bending stuff. Makes me think."

"Me, I loved running but I ran over grass and fences," said Ozzie. "Oh, I truly loved it. I love the roar of the crowd." The steeplechaser beamed.

Sneaky Pie teased the handsome Thoroughbred: "I like running under fences."

"We horses make a lot of money, and I don't even know what we bring in through spectator spending. People pay at the gate, they buy food, and at tracks like Keeneland there are wonderful clothes and stuff you can buy. I don't know if anyone knows that, but just the Kentucky Horse Park alone brings in two hundred fifty-one million dollars each year. That's a lot of oats—certainly nothing to sneeze at."

"Very impressive."

"State horse parks do a lot. Virginia's center in Lexington is always busy. The Carolina Horse Park brings in thirteen million dollars, and then you go to places like Palm Beach Polo and its International Equestrian Center, and they generate maybe eighty million dollars a year."

"That's a lot of revenue," Sneaky remarked, and Dixie raised his head.

"One-point-nine billion dollars in taxes to all levels of government," Dixie added. "I'm not as interested as Ozzie in what we do for the human economy, but I remember people back in Kentucky talking about taxes. I don't really understand taxes."

"I don't, either." The cat sat between the two horses. "It's a human thing."

"They fight over it," Ozzie remarked.

"The C.O. likes to do research, and every now and then I'll hear her explode about how income taxes are unconstitutional," said Sneaky. "If another human even mentions the subject, it sets her off. She's wrong about a lot, but on this sub I'm with her: Income taxes make no sense."

"How'd they pay for government before 1913?" Dixie asked.

"Customs took care of a lot of it. I also remember her saying that before 1861, the U.S. government flourished with customs money and the South paid seventy-five percent of those duties but only received twenty-five percent back. Doesn't make sense to me."

Both horses shook their heads. "How can you take money from those who earned it?" said Dixie. "What good does it do?"

"Builds the interstate roads, bridges, stuff like that. Weapons for defense. Other than that, looks like theft to me." Ozzie watched a jet trail high overhead.

"Like I said, it's a human thing, and whoever is in power lies about it," said Sneaky. "Doesn't matter if it's state or nation. I think it's a little harder to lie at the county level, because your neighbors tend to know where you live."

This made them all laugh.

"I can tell you one thing." Ozzie looked back at the two friends. "Horses are the future, not the past."

"Why do you say that?" asked Sneaky. She felt that cats also had a bright future.

"The Chinese." Ozzie took a deep breath and dramatically declared: "Horse City! The Chinese are building a horse city. They plan on training eight thousand people to work with horses there."

"You're kidding." Dixie couldn't fathom that.

"It's all true," swore Ozzie. "They've got to find quality stallions because they want to breed a thousand of them for an eight-hundred-twenty-three-acre park in Tianjin. They don't have really good horses, as I'm sure you know. Well, anyway, they intend to make horse feed, veterinary stuff. They say they will build luxury hotels at this city to promote horse tourism. I mean, the plan just goes on and on. They swear that within five years, it will bring millions upon millions of dollars to the area, and ultimately the country, as the horse business expands. And that doesn't take into account all the salaries of the thousands of people who will find employment as Horse City takes off."

"Ozzie, that's fantastic." Sneaky Pie meant fantastic as hard to believe. Now that she was interested in politics, she found it important to be perfectly understood.

"They aren't stupid. The Chinese know the money that's made from special events. The World Equestrian Games brought in three hundred eleven million dollars in Aachen, Germany, and we just had it here in the U.S. last year. Two hundred five million dollars just from the games in Kentucky."

"Wonder if the Russians will do the same thing?" Sneaky thought out loud. "They used to be great horsemen."

"Whenever human governments crash or millions die in revolutions, a lot of that from starvation, not just war killing, all animal life is imperiled. Yes, the Russians used to be extraordinary horsemen," Ozzie said with conviction. "But the Chinese know horses are the future. Remember, millions of Chinese humans are now making money hand over fist. And jobs plus horses exude an allure, don't you agree? The Chinese want all that goes with it. Some businessman makes a bundle trading in Shanghai, next thing you know, he buys horses to impress his friends. Hires a trainer. The whole nine yards." Ozzie could see it all unfold in his equine imagination.

"I sure hope they take good care of them," Dixie noted.

"They have an equestrian association, but they really have to learn everything all over again," Ozzie said.

"Americans never forgot." Sneaky Pie smiled. "Oh, fewer folks know horses than they once did, say, in 1900, but plenty still do. It's a passion passed down through families. But maybe, like the Chinese, someone gets money in the pot, and they court the allure of owning horses. Hey, just the smell of saddles and bridles alone is worth it." Sneaky laughed.

The two Thoroughbreds laughed, too, and the tiger cat bid them good afternoon. Walking back to the house, she became more and more excited about animals working together.

She was sure the key to success was money—not political graft but good old-fashioned American capitalism.

CHAPTER 13

Hanging Out

At 2:30 A.M., forty-mile-an-hour winds (with sixty-mile-an-hour gusts) hit the house like Thor's fist. Despite double-glazed windows, the wind whistled through the tiniest apertures. It whooshed down chimneys, throwing fine soot up from the fireplaces into the air.

Sneaky Pie, asleep on the C.O.'s pillow, awakened with a start. Pewter was out cold on the other pillow. Below, on the rug by the bed, the two dogs also opened their eyes.

"That shook the whole house," Tucker remarked.

"Been a long time since we've had wind like that." Sneaky stretched, jumped off the bed.

"Come on." Tally led the way to the kitchen. Outside the windows, the sky was pitch black.

"Here comes the rain." Tucker was startled for a moment when the rain smacked the house with force. "It's like it's come all at once. No lead-up."

"Strange." Tally listened to the wind rattle the shutters on the windows. "We're going to have a lot to clean up tomorrow."

"At least the horses, and Addie and Great Bess, will be all right," Sneaky noted. "They've got their run-in sheds."

"Half the time they stand out in the rain." Tucker shook her head. "Once I asked Addie why she did that, and she said the rain felt good on her heavy coat. Rinsed the dirt and dust out."

"She can always swim in the river," Tally said.

"The cows do sometimes. The horses go in the river, in the pond, and in the water troughs, but I bet they're not out in this mess," Tucker observed. As she was speaking, the sky lit up hot pink, a blinding flash followed by a roar of thunder that must have sounded like the huge cannon, Big Bertha, in World War I.

All three animals jumped.

"Where'd you go?" Pewter skidded into the room, eyes wide. "You left me!"

"You were dead to the world," Sneaky Pie informed her.

Pewter jumped onto the counter, peered out the

kitchen window over the sink. "Black as the devil's eyebrows."

Just then another searing flash caused her to blink and move away from the window. A tremendous clap of thunder sounded directly overhead. It seemed the sky was falling.

"Good Lord," Tucker exclaimed.

"That hurt my eyes." Pewter jumped down to the floor.

"It does, doesn't it?" Sneaky Pie agreed.

The rain lashed on the house so loudly, the thunder boomed so steadily, that the four animals didn't hear human footsteps padding down the hall.

Pewter ran to the C.O., rubbing on her leg. "I'm scared."

"All right, Pewter." The human picked up the rotund kitty, who hid her face in the person's neck. She clicked on the lights. Walking to the porch, she switched on the outside light. The rain was so heavy, there was nothing to be seen.

"Mother, it's going to be a big day tomorrow," Tucker said, preparing her for the work ahead.

"Let's check the basement." The C.O. opened the door, wooden steps reverberating as she descended, followed by the three animals.

Pewter remained on her shoulder.

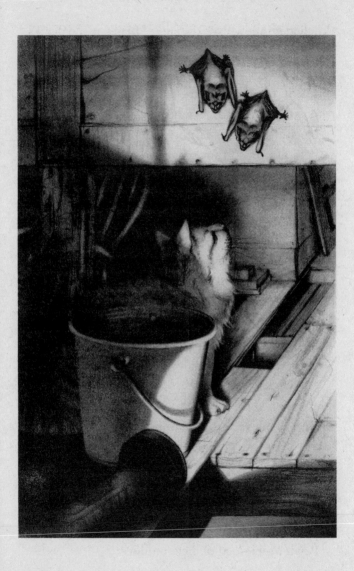

Tally ran over to the puddle forming in a corner of the basement. "Roof's leaking again."

"Dammit. Dammit to hell." The C.O. put Pewter down on a low table there, grabbed a bucket kept for this purpose, and put it where the water dripped. "Come on."

They hurried back upstairs, the thunder deafening as their human grabbed a powerful flashlight from a kitchen drawer. Down the hall they trotted, Pewter bringing up the rear.

Pulling a stepladder out of the hall closet, the C.O. set it up under a trapdoor, climbed up, and lifted the heavy door, propping it open.

She shined the light around before descending again. Hurrying into the kitchen, she pulled out a bucket from under the sink, returned, and climbed up again with bucket and flashlight. The cats were already in the attic, as were many bats hanging upside down.

"Cats," one of the bats warned the others.

"Don't worry. We're here to fix the leak," Pewter thoughtfully said.

"You won't fix it tonight." A second bat swung a little upside down as he watched the human hoist herself up onto the attic floor.

"The bucket should catch the worst of it," said

Sneaky. "Tomorrow she'll get up on the roof, unless it's too wet."

The C.O. beheld all the bats. "Too much rain for you all, too," she said as she walked over to the drip, constant and strong now.

Sneaky looked up where the flashlight beam revealed a tear. "The wind did it. Tore a little piece of the tin roof right off."

The human said nothing, positioned the bucket, and shivered a bit. The temperature had dropped.

"Will she kill us later?" another bat asked the cats. "Now that she's seen us?"

"No," Sneaky assured them. "She likes you all. You, Barn Swallows, Tree Swallows, and Purple Martins eat so many insects. You're safe."

"How unusual." The second bat stopped swinging. "Most humans fear us."

"She knows better," Pewter called up.

"Interesting," the first bat remarked. "People think we'll tangle in their hair or give them rabies."

"Makes me so mad," the second bat complained. "We don't have any more rabies than possums or raccoons, but we get blamed for everything."

"Humans are afraid of the dark. You all fly in ziggy ways. You're night creatures. It's the way they're made," Sneaky sagely noted. "Listen. I want to change the subject. I am going to run for president, and I'm hoping you will help me."

Not one bat said a word. They just hung there.

Pewter nudged Sneaky. "Maybe they don't know what a president is."

"We know," the third bat responded. "What a terrible job."

"Yes, I suppose it is," said Sneaky, "but it will take a nonhuman to solve the really big problems: food, water, depleting the soil. That kind of stuff. The humans have lost their way. They talk about the environment, but they don't really live in it, you know what I mean?" Sneaky was getting revved up again.

"I believe that," said Bat Number Three. "Do you see how bright their cities are at night? We don't even fly into Crozet, there's so much light. We've heard there are enormous cities, millions of people, and those places are lit up all night."

"It's true," said Pewter. "The energy consumed is wasteful. It's one thing if the electricity comes from Niagara Falls, but most electricity does not." Pewter didn't like electricity one bit.

"Why do they do this? Live in light like that? Doesn't that disturb their sleep?" The first bat just couldn't understand this.

"Like I said, they're afraid of the dark," Sneaky repeated.

"They're afraid of one another." Pewter accurately identified the problem. "Who could blame them?"

"Ah," all the bats said in unison and swung a bit as another mighty clap of thunder rattled the windows, winds buffeting the attic.

"Do this for me," said Sneaky. "I will represent you as best I can. I don't know how much money you save humans by eating insects, but I'm sure this insect eradication is immensely valuable. I don't think they've ever calculated it." Sneaky looked up at them, all of their beady eyes raptly attentive. "Night creatures and day creatures live different lives on different schedules. Will you discuss my campaign with raccoons, all the owls, possums, Whip-poor-wills? Talk to all the night animals? I need everyone's support."

"We will," the first bat promised.

"Kitty cats, come on." The C.O. was backing down the ladder. She couldn't care less that their conversation wasn't yet ended, but they dutifully followed.

The two cats walked to the opening. Pewter looked down as the human reached the floor and put down the flashlight. "I am not backing down a ladder."

Seeing two cats looking down at her, the C.O. got the drift. She climbed back up, lifted Pewter onto her shoulder, climbed down. Sneaky had turned around to back down the ladder just as the house's power shut off with a *crack*.

"Damn, damn, double damn," the human cursed.

The tiger cat reached the ground. The human picked up the flashlight, climbed back up. Then, putting the flashlight in the pocket of her frayed robe, she slid the attic cover closed with difficulty.

"Good night, bats," she called, as she lowered the wooden cover.

" 'Night," they called back.

CHAPTER 14

Woodpeckers for More Bugs,
Less Chemicals

The sun just cleared the horizon as Sneaky Pie, Tucker, Tally, and the C.O. loaded up the ATV with a chain saw, a chain, and heavy limb clippers.

As the four-wheel machine, built for farm chores and hunting, puttered to life, the C.O. slipped on heavy gloves, shifted out of neutral, into first, let out the clutch, and slowly rolled down the road between the barns as little rivulets ran below. Sneaky observed while riding in the front basket.

The dogs raced behind. They didn't have far to run, because at the bottom of the hill, between two paddocks, a pine tree had fallen across the gouged-out driveway. Beyond that, the animals could see that the culvert under the little earthen bridge was jammed full of debris, water subsiding so it no longer rolled over the road.

"Bet the big bridge has branches and logs sticking all the way to the other end of that culvert," Tucker surmised.

"That's why she brought the chain." Sneaky Pie moved to the backseat as the human pulled out the chain saw.

"This little thing can't pull a tree trunk," Tally noted, sniffing the ATV.

"Can pull out branches." Tucker peered into the muddy waters racing under the small culvert, getting backed up on the upside bank. "That will get more water through the culvert, and some debris might get pushed out. We'll see what it is when we get down there. Who knows what's in the road?"

"We've got a mile and a half of dirt road." Sneaky was good at calculating distances. "Lot of wind. Lot of water. The sun should help, but a little wind would, too. Not that it should blow as bad as last night, but anything to help dry up this mess."

The C.O. started up the chain saw, pulling the cord. She began cutting through the tree trunk at an angle and up. One couldn't falter in concentration for a second, which was one reason to cut up, not down. She had explained all of this to Sneaky, who usually enjoyed her human creature's lectures on various topics, though now and again, when Mother was properly riled up, Sneaky actually wished she'd keep her opinions to herself. Sometimes the chain saw, heavier once the task is completed, fools the person using it and drops farther down than he realized, cutting through a thigh, usually. If one slices upward and at an angle, a nasty injury is often avoided. Being far out in the country, state roads possibly blocked, a chain-saw accident in these conditions would probably mean the human would bleed to death before help could arrive, plus the ambulance crew would have to clear the farm road to get in. Country humans knew these things. People moving to rural areas for the beauty often did not. With amusement, Sneaky had observed the C.O. trying to help newcomers, but so many of them, successful and important in the cities from which they'd fled, disregarded her friendly advice. Mother was what was known as a redneck. The result of ignoring her proffered counsel was overturned tractors, burned-out clutches in trucks, and new tires at too frequent intervals.

These days she kept her mouth shut, welcomed people, stayed friendly but offered not one word, of course. The animals, on the other hand, never kept their traps shut, lording their superior knowledge over the pampered pooches from the city.

The sound of the chain saw changed as it bit into the living tree trunk, the smell of its wood so different from that of a dead tree. It was a pleasant scent, but the chain saw's grating roar was irksome, so the three animals decided to walk over to the Rockfish River and its formerly quiet pool. After last night's storm, the river was raging.

Tucker had heard tell of the rockfish. "Think he's down there in all that swirl?"

"I don't know," said Tally. "Bet he's sheltered under a rock overhang or tree roots where lots of bank has washed away." Tally thought of how a fish could hide from roiling waters.

"That rockfish is scrappy. He'll survive," called the Downy Woodpecker, not so high up in a walnut tree near the bank.

"Guess he will," Tucker replied. "We all learn what we need to know."

"Most of us do," the Downy Woodpecker agreed, "though the ones who don't learn never live to tell the tale. Where's that fat gray cat?"

Sneaky laughed. "Pewter recognized her duty in time to avoid it."

"Maybe that's why she's fat." The sunlight caught the bright red part of the Downy Woodpecker's head.

They all laughed.

"Seen any of the cowbirds lately?" Sneaky asked.

"Out and about," replied the colorful winged creature. "They like to sit on the backs of Great Bess and Addie. They gossip around the clock, those birds."

"Have you thought any more about supporting my bid for president?" Sneaky asked.

"As a matter of fact, I have," replied the bird, a bit formally. "You've got my vote, but I don't think you'll get block support from us birds. It's too controversial. Supporting a feline must be an individual choice for every bird. There's too much history of cats killing songbirds. And of course the cowbirds hate your guts. The raptors will support you, but you all think more alike than different. They do what you do but from the air. The strategies are the same." Clearly, the Downy Woodpecker had given all this a lot of thought.

Sneaky was grateful. "Thank you for telling me this. I appreciate your support."

Tally called up to the bird. "Don't you believe Sneaky should have a Jack Russell for her running mate?"

The woodpecker's answer was forcefully delivered: "No."

"Tally, give it up," Tucker advised.

The lovely bird let out its distinctive call before

saying "While I admire your motives and applaud your efforts, I still don't think you can accomplish very much."

"Might I know why you'd say such a thing?" Sneaky inquired. She thought it good policy to listen to her critics. Dialogue often yielded unexpected benefits.

"Well," the woodpecker started, "even if you win, you have to work with what humans call vested interests. They are powerful, motivated by money or, in some cases, laziness. They will fight you tooth and nail. How can you buy them off?"

"I can't," the cat honestly replied. "I can only hope that enough sheer animal power allied with the humans will overwhelm them, and they have to work for the common good."

"Never happen," the bird squawked pessimistically. "Huge special interests are out only for themselves."

"I agree," said Tally, still upset not to be considered vice-presidential material. The Jack Russell actually did think about some things, contrary to popular opinion.

"You do what you have to do," the midsized bird said, encouraging the cat, "but let me give you one little example from the world of woodpeckers. When we show up in large numbers in any location, it means the trees are infested. There are always bugs in trees, but when we woodpeckers gather among a farmer's cultivated trees, that means the farmer will lose his crop. So what do they do? They spray. I see it all the time. This nasty poison hurts us, and it does them not a bit of good. By the time they identify the problem of bugs, the trees are already well on their way to dying."

Sneaky wanted to clarify the woodpecker's position. "You're saying no chemicals?"

"Yes. Let the trees die. They will anyway. Cut them down. Use them for sawdust. Even if us woodpeckers get most all the bugs from the trees, the damage has been done. So core out the roots or pull up the stumps, let the land rest for a couple of years. After that, the humans can either turn it back into a pasture or try again with a different species of tree. All too often I see them replanting without enough thought. All they're doing is creating more food for those same bugs years down the line."

"Wouldn't the solution be to kill the larvae?" Tucker couldn't imagine eating bugs, but then the woodpecker couldn't imagine rolling in decayed flesh.

"That's not as easy as you would think," said the bird. "The larvae survive when the tree is alive.

Then they hatch and eat the tree. When the tree is dead, the bugs are done with it. Not every single kind of bug works that way, but most do. The thing I'm telling you, *Madame* Candidate, is that there are no short-term solutions to certain problems. Unless our forests are completely denuded, I personally will always have something to eat. The whole issue does raise the rather interesting question: What's a good bug and what's a bad bug?"

"A ladybug is a good bug." Tally liked them. They were cute.

"Until there are far too many." Tucker was catching on to the Downy's drift. "No human wants to see too many ladybugs crawling across her screened windows."

"Right," agreed the bird. "We can all agree that Japanese beetles are bad. Boll weevils are bad, but any bug can break bad, if you know what I mean. Well, it's the same with some animals. If you have an overpopulation, things go to hell in a hurry."

"I understand." Tucker did.

"So if we see swarms of you, problems," Tally said.

"Listen for our calls," said the bird. "During spring, you'll hear all the different woodpeckers calling to one another. Then it quiets down, and mostly what you hear are territory claims, some fussing at a nest occasionally. The trees are fine. They live and die like we do. Some trees live for centuries—pines, thirty years. I mean, the loblollies—those kinds, the ones really susceptible to bugs—are short-lived. Hardwoods usually last longer than pines, and they will get some insects, not so many damaging ones. I usually eat ants on hardwoods; some butterflies and moths place their chrysalids on branches. I'll eat those, too, but really, hardwoods are pretty safe. Humans should avoid all their sprays and potions. You can try and outsmart nature, but you won't succeed."

"Mom says once chestnuts were everywhere, then they got sick and died," Sneaky recalled. "All of them."

"Before my time." The bird opened one wing while leaving the other at his side. It felt good to stretch.

"Turn of the last century," the tiger cat informed him. "But you're right, I'm sure. Bugs seem to prefer certain species."

"Cultivated tastes." The bird laughed at his pun.

The other animals did, too, then turned at the sound of the human's ATV starting up. Always making a racket, the humans could be as noisy as any animal.

"She made short work of that." The Downy Woodpecker admired hard labor. "The culvert, too."

Tucker smiled. "She's covered in mud."

"I don't think our human will ever make the cover of *Vogue*!" Tally smiled, too.

"Might make the cover of *The Progressive Farmer*." Sneaky thought that would be just wonderful, especially if she was featured in the photo in the C.O.'s arms.

That would win the farm vote!

CHAPTER 15

A Warrior's Death

The next day dawned clear. At 6:00 A.M., the mercury already nudged 54°F. The day looked promising. The roadwork and cleaning out the small culverts had been accomplished by the C.O. herself.

The animals scooted out of the house as the human headed for the barn, low mist obscuring the pastures, the honking of geese rising through the mists as the noisy birds chatted, waddled this way and that, and ate.

Each night before retiring, the human checked the water buckets in the barns, the water troughs outside. As the nights were warm, most of the horses could stay outside, though. She always brought in the two blind horses, the pony, and one-eyed Jones.

Upon hearing the house cats come in, the barn cats raced across the hayloft.

"What are you all doing up there?" Sneaky called.

"Morning exercise," the black-and-white cat, Dezi, announced. "Come on up and join us."

"Later." Sneaky walked beside Tucker as the two animals checked the feed room.

A cat could never be too sure about mice. Those sharp rodent front teeth could chew through the thickest wood. For this reason, all the food bins had been lined in zinc. Special feeds were poured into metal garbage cans. Still, the ever-crafty mice might make progress if a tiny hole inadvertently appeared in a garbage can. This was usually caused by a sharp object just nicking the side as it fell from human hands. Then those mice would worry that little spot because the luscious odor of the commercial feed filled the air. Mostly, though, the mice relied on the folded feed bags, tied up with twine, then carried to the dump once a week.

Chewing the back end of those bags off was easy. The reward was sweet tidbits.

Tucker frowned. "They've been here. I smell them."

Tally trotted into the feed room. "Bet we have the fattest mice in Virginia." Then she looked at Pewter, who had joined them. "Speaking of which, the fattest cat, too."

Pewter unleashed a straight right to the jaw. "Creep."

"Ouch!"

"The only reason you're thin is you haven't been spayed, an event the rest of us pray for daily. You'll blow up like a broody hen when you're fixed," Pewter predicted.

"You say." The Jack Russell took a precautionary step backward.

Leaving the feed room, Sneaky called up to the barn cats. "Hey, you guys aren't catching any mice. They've chewed the bottoms off the feed bags."

Dezi replied, "Well, Pewter gets into them, too, but the bags are empty. We'd kill the mice if they messed with full ones, but the C.O. always dumps them in the bins or the cans. We aren't lazy."

This declaration was followed by a loud grunt, then the *click* of a bill as the barn owl up in the cupola let out a laugh.

The barn cats looked upward, wisely refraining from an argument. These barn cats were a wild lot, to be sure, but they knew better than to sass the powerful owl.

Sneaky followed Jones, Blue Sky, and Shamus as the C.O. led them out of their special paddock.

The dogs tagged along, too. Pewter reposed on a fleece saddlepad in the tack room. She felt she'd had enough exercise for the day, and it wasn't yet seven o'clock!

Each horse was turned around to face the human. She patted them on the neck, then their halters were slipped off. Then the three horses whirled to run to the end of the paddock. Despite the visual limitations of Blue Sky and Shamus, their senses were so keen they knew the dimensions of the paddock. They never ran into the fence or into each other. Eager to be free this glorious morning, when the human opened the gate, Jones, Blue Sky, and Shamus happily loped into the early sunshine.

The cats and dogs ambled through that pasture into the next. When all the gates were opened to the other upper pastures, the horses could enjoy thirty acres with varied terrain, watered by a strong running creek. With his one good eye showing the way, Jones still surely loved to gallop. Disappearing over the hill, he then came charging back up.

Before she slipped under the fence, Sneaky turned just in time to see Jones stumble. She waited for a moment. He recovered, then went down again.

"Hurry!" the tiger cat yelled to her friends.

They rushed to the aged horse. He lay on his side, his breathing rapid and shallow.

Tucker licked the old fellow's nose. "Jones, Jones, are you all right?"

"Ah." He blew out from his nostrils. "My legs don't want to work."

Tally hit the turbo, turning tail and running for the human. She was puttering in the tractor shed.

Sneaky sat by Jones's head, his large brown eyes soft. "Do you hurt?"

"No. I feel weak." A deep breath followed this. "Pussycat, my dear friend, my time has come. Sit with me awhile. You, too, Tucker."

"We won't leave," Tucker reassured the horse, as she saw the human running toward them, Tally leading the way.

The C.O. knelt beside Jones, pulling back his lips to look at his gums. She placed her fingers on the big vein running along his neck.

"Jones, I'll call the vet." The C.O. met Sneaky's eyes: Both of them knew he was dying. The human didn't want the beloved horse to suffer.

"No need," Jones whispered. "Don't trouble yourself."

She ran to the tack room of the barn as the three animals sat with Jones. Hearing the C.O.'s call, Pewter jumped off the saddlepad and hurried to her friends.

"Jones, don't die," Pewter wailed, as Sneaky shot her a sharp "shut up" look.

"We all have to go sometime," the old Thoroughbred replied with great sense.

The horses in the other pasture trotted up to the fence line.

Jones lifted his head. "Ozzie, you'll be the oldest now. Keep them in line."

Blue Sky walked up, Shamus by his side, as the pony depended on the Saddlebred more than the other way around. Each of Jones's paddock mates nuzzled him.

Shamus let out a high nicker. "Jones, what will we do without you?"

"Live." Jones laid his head back down, for it felt so heavy. "You'll go on."

"I'll take care of things," the blind Saddlebred promised.

"I know." Jones breathed faster now. "You all look after the human. I've been with her over half her life. She needs all the horse sense you can give her. She has a good heart. Promise me."

They all promised, and Tally started to sob in anguish.

Pretty soon the barn cats came down to say goodbye, as did the barn swallows. Jones had lived so long that generations of barn swallows knew him.

All the animals knew him. He'd always been there, like the mountains.

The human came back, a towel over her shoulders. She sat on the grass beside her oldest animal friend.

"It will be okay, buddy." She rubbed the towel over his face and along his neck, hoping it would feel good.

"You saved me. You've saved a lot of us," Jones managed to say. "I've had a good life. Thank you for it." He raised his head slightly, looked at her, then laid it down.

The gathering of friends waited. Fortunately, the vet was on call in the area, reaching them within a half hour.

Fading fast, Jones heard the truck tires. "Sneaky Pie, don't ever stop fighting for what's right. You can still save the animals."

The cat rubbed her head on his. "I won't," she said sadly.

The vet calmly walked down the hill, sensitive not to frighten the other horses. She placed her hand on the C.O.'s shoulder.

"Thanks for getting here so fast, Anne."

The vet knelt down beside Jones, checked him out. "His systems are shutting down."

"I don't want him to suffer."

Anne walked back up to her truck, filling a syringe as the C.O. slipped halters back over Blue Sky and Shamus. The human walked the two blind horses back to their stalls.

When she rejoined Anne, the C.O. stroked Jones's head.

Tally really wailed now.

"Tally, I can't see you anymore, but I sure can hear you," Jones rasped, and Sneaky couldn't help it, she laughed.

Then Jones was gone.

The animals stayed at his side as the humans walked up to the barn.

Two hours later, Burly Connick drove up the farm road with his ditch witch and began to dig a deep hole.

Sneaky and the human watched as he prepared to push the body in. The C.O. climbed up on the machine so he could hear her, hanging on to the bars. "Burly, lay him out so he faces the mountains. He loved the mountains."

And it was done.

As she paid Burly, the man said, "You two been together a long time."

"Yes, we were, over thirty years."

"My little Trixie," he named his dachshund, now departed, "lived to fifteen, and when she died I cried like a baby. A baby." He reached for the chew in his pocket with one hand as he took the check with the other. "I think they know more than we do."

"Yes" was all the C.O. managed to say.

And, for once, Pewter stayed quiet.

CHAPTER 16

Literary Aspirations Revealed

A week had passed since Jones died. All the animals continued to mourn him; he'd been in his pasture since each one had been born. Everyone felt low. The human said nothing but carried a handkerchief to dab her eyes.

This last Saturday in May, everyone but Pewter worked on farm repairs. You'd cross two chores off your list and three new ones would hop on the bottom.

Sneaky used the sad time to canvass more animals. She'd talked to the Canada geese, the chickens (impossible twits), the muskrats, any and all whom she encountered. Every now and then the cowbirds continued their bombing campaign, but they didn't show up in full force, for which everyone was grateful.

Alone in the house, Pewter had the computer all to herself. Furious that over the years she had been portrayed as a fat, self-involved diva, she was determined to write a smash novel of her own. The computer was really easy to use. The cat couldn't understand why they used an apple for a logo. Made no sense. She thought it should be a jet or a cheetah running flat out. A cat never could tell what logos or totems would motivate people.

The human had helpfully supplied the electronic mouse with little ears, eyes, whiskers, and a rubber tail, which amused Pewter as she moved around the device. The gray cat cackled as she worked:

> *Fangs glowing neon white, eyes burning bright, the vampire cats attacked the terrified Great Dane. The large dog ran for his life, but the vampire cats, knowing no fatigue, would eventually wear him down.*
>
> *The eastern sky lightened. They'd been running for hours. A church bell rang out, heralding the dawn.*
>
> *The vampire cats froze.*
>
> *"Back to Hell Hall," their leader commanded. The twenty cats turned to the north. They'd*

just reach the crumbling once-grand estate
before the sun cleared the horizon. . . .

So intent was Pewter on her opus that she didn't hear Sneaky softly come into the room.

Hoping Pewter was doing research on animal profits, the tiger cat leapt onto the desk.

However, when she edged over to the computer, Pewter quickly saved her work, then hastily cleared the screen.

"Pewts, what are you doing?"

"Nothing."

"Why don't I believe you?"

"*U-m-m.*" Pewter fudged. "I'm looking up things."

"Wildlife stuff?"

Fortunately, Pewter actually had looked up information concerning how much money fishing and hunting licenses brought into states. However, once alone and certain her buddies wouldn't come back, she then returned to her novel. Sneaky Pie wasn't the only literary cat. Pewter dreamed of literary fame, too. She could also imagine her vampire cat saga as a feature film. But who would star?

"Uh-huh," she stammered. "Fishing and hunting licenses for 2011 brought in $783,958,245 for the nation." She pulled up the computer screen with her research.

"That's just licenses?" The tiger cat sat on her haunches. "Easy money."

"Sure is. All each state has to do is give the person a piece of paper with the year marked on it. No service, no nothing. Any idiot can do that."

"True, but there are people who want to stop those activities." Sneaky peered more closely at the screen. "Colorado sells the most licenses. *Hmm*. Let's see." They pulled up the information gathered by the U.S. Fish and Wildlife Service. "Virginia makes almost fifteen million dollars. We should make more."

"That's what the C.O. says." Pewter had heard the human talk about fish and wildlife management ad nauseam.

However, even if she pontificated to excess, the domesticated animal did listen. Pewter wasn't so stupid as not to realize there was a connection between managing wildlife and taking care of domestic animals. The important thing was for humans to recognize their impact on all animals. Sometimes they did. Mostly, they didn't.

"Hey, look at Wyoming," Sneaky said. "It has the least number of humans in the country, but the state makes $28,395,536. Somebody's thinking straight in their state government. Mother always says state government has to solve problems. Federal government just prints more money."

"I suppose," Pewter murmured. "You've got me thinking about things differently now. This huge national figure of $783,958,245 is found money, gold on the ground. You simply pick it up. It also doesn't reflect the revenue spent by wildlife enthusiasts. Some of that stuff is really expensive."

Sneaky Pie chimed in, "They spend money on stays in motels or special camps, on food, trucks, buying four-wheel-drive vehicles. The list goes on and on. However, fishing and wildlife means clean money. No pollution. Let's start there."

"Well, I did check some of the surrounding income. The estimate on that kind of money is one-hundred-twenty-two-point-three billion dollars," Pewter proudly revealed.

"Wow. Pewter, this is incredible. Take that figure and the seventy-four billion dollars the cattle industry brings in annually and those two things alone make one-hundred-ninety-six-point-three billion dollars. I haven't even added into account what chickens, turkeys, goats, hogs produce. It's overwhelming. With these figures, I don't see how anyone—human or otherwise—could resist my commonsense arguments."

"Money talks. Bullshit walks. That's what our human says." Pewter laughed.

"Then I was thinking some more about our conversation with the Downy Woodpecker, a small fellow by woodpecker standards, but he is bigger than a house wren. In our country, there are twenty-two kinds of woodpeckers, although people say the Ivory-billed Woodpecker is extinct. I know I've never seen one, but who knows, let's hope there are a few out there. Anyway, twenty-two kinds of birds that eat bugs from trees. There are the swallows and bats, and plenty of birds who eat on the wing, catching bugs as they fly. Bugs or not, all those creatures protect the food supply."

"Sneaky, this is too big for us. You need a campaign team with paid researchers, publicity people, media experts. We're just two simple farm cats and two farm dogs."

"And Mr. Jefferson was one man," said Sneaky. "Sojourner Truth was one woman. They never gave up. And when Sojourner Truth started walking from town to town to tell her truth, who could have known she would inspire people to this day? Every movement starts with one voice decrying injustice. America recognizes only human effort. Well, I'm only one cat, but I will be heard."

"Sneaky, we don't have any money. All this research has shown me that you can be the best candidate with the best ideas in the nation—if you aren't funded, if you don't have a good staff, you aren't going to make it."

"That doesn't mean I can't shake things up. I can make change." A determined look crossed the tiger cat's face.

Footsteps alerted them. Pewter turned off the computer.

"Hi."

The two cats meowed as the C.O., tired, walked into the room.

"Are you two hungry?"

"Fresh tuna! Delmonico steak! Mouse tartare!" Pewter rapturously replied.

"Give me one minute. Just one minute." The human sat down, clicked on the computer, looked to select what she wanted, saw something unfamiliar, and pulled that up. She read aloud: *"Fangs glowing neon white, eyes burning bright, the vampire cats attacked the terrified Great Dane."* The human jumped back in alarm as Pewter flew off the desk.

Sneaky, bewildered, looked into the C.O.'s eyes.

"I must be losing my mind," the human said, looking back again at the words on the screen.

The tiger cat jumped off the desk, following Pew-

ter's scent. The fat gray cat had scooted out the back animal door.

"What's with her?" In the kitchen, Tucker lifted her head. She'd been napping on the floor after the morning's chores.

Sneaky zipped out the animal door in time to see Pewter fleeing to the old springhouse.

Within a minute, Sneaky slipped through the old wooden door, slightly ajar. She was greeted with the fresh scent of cool springwater running through the sluice.

"Leave me alone." Pewter sniffed.

Sneaky was incredulous. "Vampire cats?"

Pewter shot back, "Why not? It's vampire everything. You think you're so hot. Well, I will write the *smash* book of the year. Vampire cats! I've done some research of my own. Thirty-nine million people, give or take, have a cat or cats. That's a lot of potential readers. Plus, there are other people who like cats. My potential fan base is enormous. I'm a celebrity waiting to happen. I'll be rich as Midas!"

"Before your close-up, you might want to shed a few pounds," cracked Sneaky. "And just because there are those kinds of numbers doesn't mean those humans read."

"Vampires," Pewts enthused. "Everyone these

days wants to read about vampires. And a movie deal will surely follow. Oh, I can just see the vampires with their long fangs, glowing green eyes. And then the screams of their victims! Blood dripping off the fangs. *Vampire cats*. I'm telling you!" Pewter became quite excited. It was alarming. "Furthermore, I'm sick of being portrayed as a fat diva!"

"You take it too personally." Sneaky demurred because she did indeed think Pewter a very fat diva.

"I'm not even putting you in my book. You will not be a featured character. My cats will be deep thinkers, world travelers—not some hick tiger cat."

"Fine." Sneaky sighed. "Come on, Mother's making chicken sandwiches, and that means fresh chicken."

"You're trying to trick me."

"Pewter, if you want to stay here in the springhouse, go right ahead. If you want to write about vampire cats, go for it, Tolstoy. I hope it works. Good luck to you. It's a rough business. I just hope when you hit it big, you'll contribute to my campaign. You've already been a big help at my side on my listening tour."

"Don't forget my research." Pewts pouted.

"Yes, I was just getting to that." Sneaky smiled.

"Fresh chicken—truly?"

"Fresh chicken."

A spring in their steps, the cats trotted up from the little creek. Campaigning meant listening to everyone, Sneaky realized. She wasn't just one cat. She represented many and varied interests, pandering to their egos and, most important, giving credit to others for work you've done. Sneaky hoped she was equal to the challenge.

Once in the kitchen, Tally ran up to report on the C.O.: "She's muttering about vampire cats."

The trio of animals looked over at her, now slapping Duke's mayonnaise onto bread.

"You know how she gets." Pewter airily tossed this off. "Bizarre ideas pop into her head."

CHAPTER 17

One Moment in Time

During that evening's sunset, cumulus clouds turned gold, then pink to scarlet, fading to lavender with slashes of purple. It was breathtaking.

Cats, dogs, birds in their nests, the night birds preparing to forage, the foxes, bobcats, bears, deer, beavers, muskrats, and even the craven coyotes all beheld the glorious spectacle.

Humans did, too. The C.O. had phoned some of her good friends to make sure they were watching the symphony of color. With darkness came the night scents. The earth seemed more pungent, the pines sharper. The last of the fruit tree blossoms summoned up a final trumpet of sweetness.

Wearing a sweater, the human sat on the porch in an Adirondack chair badly in need of a fresh coat of paint. The usual crew gathered below on the floor. An old serviceable lantern sat on the wooden side table outside. Sneaky watched as the human lit a match, took a deep breath, then blew it out, apparently thinking better of it, a decision Sneaky agreed with. The lantern's oil gave off such a strong odor. Bad though human noses are, it seemed even the C.O. preferred the night's fresh fragrances.

They watched as the owl lifted off from the barn's cupola, circled once, then headed for the fields. Bats darted in and out. Turtles shut up for the night. Snakes crawled into their holes, as did field mice. Rabbits withdrew to their hutches. The cats could see every detail. The dogs, eyes not as good, could still perceive movement. The C.O. watched as well. Human eyes were quite good, although their night vision was weak.

A long yip followed another, rousing the C.O. "We'll never get rid of those coyotes now," she said.

"No, we won't," Tally agreed, "but I'll protect you."

"Me, too," Tucker chimed in.

"Take more than the four of us to bring down a coyote," Sneaky Pie advised. "Plus, they're never alone."

"Make that three. I'm not messing with them." Pewter hopped onto the C.O.'s lap, circled once, snuggled down.

"You all are chatty." The human smiled, then reached into her shirt pocket for a tiny flashlight the size of a BIC cigarette lighter.

She picked up a book next to the lantern.

"Hey," Pewter complained. Could she please sit still?

"Pewter, you can be so fussy." The C.O. laughed.

"All the time." Tally sighed. "You have no idea what I put up with."

"Tally, don't start. It's a lovely evening," Sneaky told the Jack Russell, and just then the barn owl called far away.

"Owls, bats, blacksnakes, swallows, you all, best friends. Can't farm without the team." Tucker smiled.

"Forget blacksnakes." Pewter was horrified.

"They eat a lot of vermin," Sneaky, now on the side table, mentioned.

"I don't care," countered Pewts. "I don't like snakes. No reptiles in your campaign. Remember?"

"I do." The tiger cat sighed.

"Just thinking of the terrible incident with that horrible snake, I shudder. I could have been killed.

A lingering, painful, terrible suffering." Pewter's pupils enlarged.

"Pewter, we know all about the snake," said Tally. "You're fine. I'm sure the copperhead is still just as scared. You might have crushed him." Tally giggled.

"Ha, ha," Pewter sarcastically said.

"I am trying to read," the human admonished them.

"That little flashlight has such a bright beam." Pewter shifted her weight, for the book was held above her head, resting on the human's knees.

"Blind. You'll be blind," Tally teased.

"Listen to this," the human said, preparing to read to them. " 'We never keep to the present. We recall the past; we anticipate the future as if we found it too slow in coming and were trying to hurry it up, or we recall the past as if to stay its too rapid flight. We are so unwise that we wander about in times that do not belong to us.' "

"True for humans." Tucker had settled on the C.O.'s boots.

"Pascal." The C.O. named the author of those words.

"Who's that?" Pewter asked.

"Someone who's been dead a long, long time," Tally replied. "She likes the old stuff."

"As long as it makes her happy," Sneaky wisely said.

"We make her happy." Pewter announced this with confidence.

"Of course we do," Tally agreed. "Animals always make people happy."

Sneaky Pie, Pewter, and Tucker stared at the little dog for a moment.

"Not always," Tucker offhandedly remarked. "Jack Russells are God's way of telling humans that not all dogs are obedient."

The animals laughed. The human looked at each of them for a moment, then went back to her book as the evening stars glowed ice white.

"We lower their blood pressure," Pewter informed them. "We calm their nerves."

Sneaky Pie curled her tail around her legs. "They're so lonely. We fight that off."

"There are so many of them," Tally said. "I mean, I suppose what you're saying is true, but I don't know how they can be lonely."

"They can't communicate with one another very well." Pewter had observed this. "They miss a lot. Misread a lot. They're not like us. We smell a lie, or fear, or attraction. They've lost their way. And they can't really read one another's bodies anymore."

"Could they ever?" asked Tucker.

"Yes, but now they rely on electronics," said Pewter. "Really." She shifted yet again in the C.O.'s lap. "They believe what's on the Internet, on their Droids. On the TV. They don't talk to one another, not like they used to. Remember when Mom was telling us about riding on the bus? She said lots of different people rode on the bus. You learned to get along. Then the rural bus lines got cut back, as well as the old train lines—little spur lines, she called them. They've lost touch with one another. It's all pulled apart. I mean people."

"I do kind of recall something about that," said Tucker. "She had a fit and fell in it over one of the presidential debates." The corgi remembered the night in front of the TV during the winter. "All that jawing on TV provoked her rant about public transportation."

Sneaky laughed. "And here she has a candidate in her own house. Just underfoot. Of course, we must get her to see that."

"Don't hold your breath." Pewter stretched, then jumped down. "Look."

They looked toward the river, a quarter of a mile away. Tiny dots of light appeared, then began moving up to the higher meadows.

"Lightning bugs." Tally jumped up, ran in a circle.

"Tally." The C.O. started to say something to

the dog, then she, too, saw the first of the flying insects. "Magic!"

The peepers sang. The owl did, too, the fireflies swirling along to their own music, it seemed. It was the true beginning of summer. The human closed her book and clicked off the flashlight.

"Doesn't get any better than this," she happily spoke, and her four friends agreed.

CHAPTER 18

Shots Are Fired

"Bubble, bubble, toil and trouble." The rockfish burped out a string of bubbles.

"Gross." Pewter stayed out of water-shot range.

"Thought I might find you in your pool now that the water is calmed." Sneaky fearlessly leaned over the creek bed.

"I have a friend with me," said the fish, disappearing, then popping back up with a catfish beside him.

The dark catfish's distinctive whiskers swayed with the slight water current. "Are you named for me, or am I named for you?" he asked Sneaky Pie.

"I don't know, but you sure are big," Sneaky said, offering a compliment.

"Lots to eat." The fish's distinctive laugh came out as a gurgle. "I'll grow even bigger," he vowed.

"I won't." The rockfish swished his tail near the water's surface. "But, hey, size has nothing to do with brains."

The catfish agreed in part. "Though you could say what's dumb dies."

"Not always." Pewter cut her eyes toward Tally, chasing butterflies nearby.

"There are exceptions to every rule." The big catfish smiled. "My friend Rocky here tells me you harbor political ambitions."

"I do," Sneaky forthrightly replied.

"He told me, I told my brethren, and the word sailed on down the line into the Chesapeake Bay. There are big fish there. And then, of course, the Bay flows into the Atlantic. The biggest fish ever swim in the ocean. Well, I can't substantiate this, but what's come back up to us is that fish aren't going to help you. They are unwilling to help humans. The Big Boys, you know, the whales, the sailfish, the hammerheads, and even the manta rays, they say the bipeds first crawled out of the ocean because the rest of them in the sea didn't want them. 'Good riddance to bad rubbish,' they say."

The tiger cat was surprised. "Really?"

"The whales are still angry over the many years of whaling, especially out of those New England towns. That was the largest industry in the nineteenth century for decades, and they aren't quick to forgive the slaughter."

The rockfish added to the catfish's report. "They're mad about *Moby-Dick*, too."

Pewter, inching closer, said, "Hey, what about *Puss 'n Boots*?"

"Pewter, the cat's the hero," Sneaky told her. "You've nothing to complain about. In *Moby-Dick*, the whale is the bad guy," the tiger informed the gray.

"I prefer to think of Moby-Dick as representing Nature," the large fish said. "Kind of an overgrown catfish." More bubbles popped on the water's surface.

Sneaky said, "Ah, but then he'd be so much better-looking, that white whale."

The catfish laughed. "You just might have a shot at a political career."

He dove back down, and the rockfish followed.

The two cats meandered through the pastures, milk butterflies everywhere, grasshoppers shooting straight up then hitting the half-grown hay with a *click, click, click.*

"Think the big fish really said that?" Pewter wondered.

"We'll never know. It might be idle gossip among chatty fish. But if they did say it, the whales have a point." Sneaky then noticed the grass. "Chickweed."

"The weed killer doesn't work on this. Kills some, but chickweed's kinda like cockroaches." Pewter giggled. "Can't get them all."

"Waterbugs," said Sneaky, diverted by the topic. "I can tolerate cockroaches, but waterbugs set me off. And spiders. They move funny."

"Boy, if insects could vote, if you could just get them interested, nobody could overcome those numbers," said Pewter. "And I still think you should talk to earthworms."

Before Sneaky could again affirm that she would not be pressing earthworms for her campaign, Tally shot past them.

"What the—?" Pewter exclaimed.

"Uh-oh!" Sneaky took a big sniff, turned her head, and saw the mother bear rumbling her way through the pasture.

Both cats hit the accelerator, following the dog.

"Hide your children!" Tally screamed to the horses. "Protect yourselves!"

Hearing the little dog's warning, the horses saw

the running bear. They could easily evade the huge animal, but the bear's presence did agitate them. They snorted and ran around.

"Momma, Momma, I'm tired," the bear cub called up to her furious mother.

The brown bear stopped. "Did that little runt dog bite you?"

"She barked a lot and came real, real close," said the little girl cub. "Oh, Momma, she near to broke my eardrums."

"Well, I'll set her straight. Come on, little one." The mother, calming down, moved slower now.

The C.O., who'd been repairing the fence, slipped the hammer through her belt.

Tucker, helping, called out to Tally, "You're okay. She won't catch you."

The cats tore up behind Tally.

Having noted the commotion, the human now saw the bear and her cub. She calmly trotted to the tack room of the barn, her animals following her.

She grabbed the shotgun leaning against the wall, slipped in two shells, and walked back outside.

When she fired in the air, Tally blasted out through the animal door in the tack room. Emboldened by the shotgun, the Jack Russell hurled insults.

"My God, she's a blistering idiot." Tucker slipped through the door to help the C.O.

The cats followed.

Racing around the human, barking as loudly as she could, the little dog would stop, take a step in the direction of the mother and cub, then race around again.

Not entirely stupid, the human yelled, "Tally, sit down."

Seeing the human and hearing the warning blast, the bear stopped. Her cub stopped with her.

"You come near my baby again and I will break your neck," said the enraged mother bear.

"You could never catch me," Tally shouted back.

"Tally, shut up!" The C.O. purposefully stepped on her small tail, eliciting a yelp.

"You'd better do what she says," Tucker warned.

Sneaky moved forward, calling to the bear, "We're sorry. Tally has ideas above her station."

"I will break her neck," the bear again warned.

"If you don't, I will," Sneaky replied, which made the bear laugh.

The human lowered her shotgun as the bear turned, rambling back down the pasture.

"*Whew,*" she said, as she broke the shotgun, taking out the shells.

Pewter said, "Ever notice how some humans look like animals?"

"Yes, I have," Sneaky replied.

Staring at the retreating bear, the gray cat quipped, "I've seen hairy butts on a few humans just like that."

The cats laughed uproariously.

"What did you do, exactly?" Tucker grilled Tally.

"Nothing."

"Tally," Tucker said sternly.

"The cub was playing, and I just snuck up. I was so quiet in my approach that I startled her. She got scared and ran for her mother."

"You barked the second you were out of your mother's womb." Pewter watched the four-hundred-pound animal move through the pastures, not the least bit interested in the horses.

Big Sky, Shamus at his side, smelled the bear. He whinnied, "Should I run?"

Ozzie replied, "No. She was mad at Tally but is leaving now. We're safe."

"Tally, you're leaving something out." Tucker stared at her friend.

"All I did was smell the cub." The Jack Russell paused. "Maybe I tugged at her fur. Just a little bit."

"Tally, you are out of your mind," said Sneaky. "This is exactly why you or any Jack Russell should never be in politics," the cat said exasperatedly. "And you likely just cost me the bear vote."

"Oh, Sneaky Pie, bull," Tally fired back. "You didn't have the bear vote."

"Well, I might have," Sneaky responded.

"Yeah!" Pewter would always take sides against Tally.

"Come on, let's call it off," Tucker advised, heading back to the tack room.

"Call off the dogs." Pewter smirked.

"Going to the dogs." Sneaky giggled, joining Pewter in his canine taunt.

"Fight like cats and dogs," Tally said, entering the fracas, racing up beside Pewter and nipping her big butt, taking with her a tiny bit of fur.

"I've been attacked!" The gray cat flopped on her side. "I'm wounded."

Sneaky examined her. "Just a hunk of fur. Don't worry. No blood. And anyway, you have eight more lives."

Pewter, mollified by the attention, thought for a moment. "That could be a campaign point. You have nine lives. The electorate need never worry about assassinations. Of course, sometimes I think one life is bad enough, especially if you have to share it with a Jack Russell."

"Right." Sneaky laughed, then took off like a shot, climbing the pin oak by the barn.

Pewter climbed right up after her. They each parked themselves in a large V where a big branch joined the trunk.

Pewter's spirits were restored. She smiled. "We're in the catbird seat."

CHAPTER 19

Saving for Tomorrow,
One Bone at a Time

"I'm getting all my ducks in a row." Sneaky Pie walked confidently beside Tucker, a light breeze sweeping over them from the northwest as they strolled along the banks of the Rockfish River.

"The good news is that the Monticello mice will support you." The corgi smiled. "Last night the C.O.'s meeting up there proved very helpful for us."

"She loves to be part of the upcoming swearing-in ceremony for new citizens. It really is beautiful. All the trees and flowers, the light shining on the back of the house. It usually makes national television."

"When the time comes, the hardest part for us will be lying low until the swearing in, but I like your plan, Sneaky. After the ceremony, the spectators leave, the new citizens walk down to the director's house for all-American hot dogs, some music. Then the podium is all yours." Tucker sat with Sneaky to watch the sunset. "But we're going to have to fool our C.O. and elude the rest."

The tiger cat observed the barn swallows darting about, heading back to their nests in the barn. "What are we going to do about Tally?"

Tucker pondered this problem. "Can't really leave her home. And she still believes she should be your running mate."

"Then there's Pewter, although she might be able to handle Tally," the cat thought out loud.

The corgi snorted. "No one can handle Tally. Plus, all those two have done since Christmas is fight."

"So much for peace on earth, goodwill to all."

"Pewter's goodwill arrives in a can of tuna." The dog laughed, then looked overhead. "Hey, it's a bald eagle."

A young male swooped low, tipped a wing as he flew down to the Rockfish River.

"Doesn't have his white hood yet," the cat remarked. "Still, eagles are impressive. I wouldn't want to tangle with one. I'm having enough trouble these days with cowbirds."

"Talons, beaks, poop." The dog laughed again. "Death from the skies!"

They both laughed as the sun dipped below a cloud to graze the top of the mountains.

"No matter how advanced technology becomes, no airplane can fly like a bird, turn, swirl, dive, climb. I suppose it's enough that people can fly, just like it's enough that they can float in a ship. I don't want to do it, do you?" Sneaky asked.

"Fly?" asked the corgi.

"Fly or sail," the cat replied.

"No, thank you. I'm built for the earth, and so are you. To every creature his or her domain."

"Right," agreed the tiger.

"Maybe it's a mistake to live outside your realm," Tucker mused.

"Maybe, but don't forget you and I ride in the truck. That machine goes faster than either of us could go on our own, so maybe airplanes and ships operate on the same principle."

"I am not going up in the air," said Tucker, before being distracted as the horizon lit up with molten gold. "I love sunsets."

"Think what it would be like to fly through those clouds," Sneaky said. "Must be beautiful."

"Well, you might be right, but I don't want to do

it." Tucker smiled. "Have you gathered all your statistics yet, to change the subject?"

"Which you brought up," said Sneaky.

"I know. That's the thing, Sneaky, you start talking or thinking and you never know where it will end up. Now, Pewter's more predictable. It's always about food."

Sneaky laughed. "Or with the C.O. She's always banging on about taxes, the cost of things. I know it's hard, but she shouldn't let it get her down."

"Taxes don't make sense. Maybe all the humans should just not pay them."

"If they did that, one by one they will be destroyed—economically, I mean. The IRS will prosecute them, confiscate their property. She better pay her taxes," said Sneaky. "I don't want to move."

Tucker quickly rejoined, "But what if it was a mass movement of thousands or millions? Just refusing to pay."

"I suppose that would do it," Sneaky said. "But more than anything, right now the humans need a leader."

"Then they can all pay their taxes and shut up about it," Tucker firmly stated.

"I agree with you there." The cat thought a long time as the sky changed from gold to scarlet right where the sun had set, hot pink toward the north but gold to the south.

She never could figure out why the color varied, nor why some sunsets produced deep colors while others filled the sky with pastels.

"You know our human is good in a crisis, but she's no politician. If someone's in trouble, though, she can get everyone together."

"Politics is poison to her," said Sneaky. "I'm the leader of the family."

"How come you don't hate politics?" asked the corgi.

The cat tilted her head for a moment. "*M-m-m*, I don't much like the cowbirds or the coyotes. I don't understand the fish. We're all animals, but they're foreign to me. Yet I don't want to see them slaughtered, I really don't. Though I don't want to work with them."

"Same for humans, I guess," said the corgi. "Some like one kind of human, some another. Now, back to taxes for a minute."

"Yes." The cat perked up her ears.

"I can't help thinking if the humans refuse to pay taxes, a whole mess of them, and instead they spent their own money fueling the economy, it will improve." The dog smiled broadly.

"That's a fact. But to be legally secure, they'd have

to put their tax liability in an account to prove they were doing just as you said. I think it's called escrow."

"That's crazy. Spend the money."

"Or they should invest," said Sneaky. She was prudent about resources, mostly from sitting with the C.O. at the desk when she tried to figure out expenses, seed and fertilizer needs, food bills, all that. "Investing means you might make money," the cat explained.

"I thought that's why humans worked," Tucker said.

"Yeah, but if a human invests, they make money off the work of other humans. Plus, their investments build companies and pay for research. It's to our own detriment that animals don't invest. It's a big weakness."

"It is not," said the corgi. "And we do invest, sort of. I bury my bones for future use. You're talking about pie in the sky. If you can't carry it in your jaws, it's useless." The dog felt one hundred percent sure on this topic. "I can dig up my bone whenever I want. What good is a piece of paper?"

"Tucker, what works for us doesn't work for them," said Sneaky. "They worry about things that happened in the past, miseries now, what can go wrong in the future. I think investing is a way to dampen all that worry."

"Like I said, pie in the sky," said the corgi. "Who knows what tomorrow will bring, or even if there will be a tomorrow? Live for today. Doesn't do you any good to tell them. That's the thing, you have good ideas, but a lot of animals have good ideas—humans don't hear them."

"I know." The tiger wrapped her tail around her as she sat. "I think I can reach our kind, especially most domesticated animals, some wild ones, I hope."

"Well, I'm all ears." The dog's pink tongue stuck out as she panted a little.

"I've been toting up sums," said Sneaky. "Pewter's helped a bunch. One-hundred-twenty-two-point-three billion dollars from hunting, fishing licenses, and ancillary costs, only partial costs, but that's the best we could do. Seventy-four billion dollars each year from cattle alone, and another three-point-five billion dollars from dairy cattle, milk, cheese, that stuff. Then you add in sheep and lambs, that's five-point-six billion dollars a year. Hogs are sixty-eight billion dollars. Chickens, turkeys, poultry are maybe one-point-six billion dollars, and horses alone are one hundred two billion dollars. The whole pet industry is about fifty-point-eighty-four billion dollars. That's four hundred billion dollars, give or take. None of this reflects the jobs created for humans by animals. None of this reflects what animals do to help humans—you know, like bats. So I would hazard a guess that our contribution to the United States economy each year has to be about one trillion dollars. I don't think we will ever truly know, but we produce revenue, jobs, and, really, health."

Tucker was astonished. "If you can ever find a way to reach humans, that number should wake them up."

"If it doesn't, can you imagine animals going on strike? Cats refusing to catch mice? Cattle running away from those trying to round them up for days? I mean, we could create far more chaos than folks withholding taxes. Why is it that people only learn through disruption and pain?"

Tucker defended their human. "Oh, our C.O. learns other ways."

"She does, I suppose, but on big political issues I don't think she's one bit different. Something hurts them, then they finally pay attention. Can you imagine what an animal strike would do, combined with a true tax revolt?"

"The government would crash and burn," Tucker soberly replied. "We don't want that."

"Quite the opposite. But sometimes one has to be destructive in order to be constructive," the tiger cat sagely noted.

"Sneaky, that's all getting over my head. You can't talk about stuff like that on the campaign trail. You'll be branded a revolutionary and be ignored. Stick to the money."

"I will. Of course, if Rush Limbaugh called me a slut, that would get more attention." She giggled.

"You're spayed." Tucker giggled back. "Your virtue is above reproach."

CHAPTER 20

Welcome to America

July 4 was blessed with sunshine and lovely cooling breezes, promising to be one of the best days ever for welcoming new citizens to the United States.

Chairs faced a dais. Also seated on the dais next to the judge who would swear in the new citizens was Leslie Bowman, the director of Monticello, the celebrity who would give a brief (it was hoped) speech to commemorate the special day.

Up in a tree with the birds, Sneaky Pie and Pewter watched as the people about to become citizens sat in the front few rows. They had been born in other nations. They were every color a human animal could be, different faiths, different ages, males and females, and who knows if there was anyone in between those two somewhat false poles of gender? Nobody cared. What mattered is that to be eligible for U.S. citizenship, these people had undergone a course of study over time. They then took a test to demonstrate they understood America's founding principles. Each person had to swear allegiance to their adopted country, to bear arms against the country of their birth, should the United States find itself at war with that nation. Such a promise, such study, required much dedication and soul-searching. It was inspirational, thought Sneaky.

The about-to-be citizens often knew the Constitution better than those who had the supreme good fortune to be born U.S. citizens.

A national treasure such as Monticello can operate only with the help of many people, people who give their money and their time. Legions of humans visited Mr. Jefferson's home in 2011, and most left with a sense of what life was like in the late eighteenth century and early nineteenth century. They took away some sense of Mr. Jefferson himself, his family, the slaves, so many of whom had highly developed skills, often promoted by the master. Slavery, sanctioned by the Old Testament, by thousands of years of human endeavor, and currently alive in parts of the world today, nonetheless left a troubling legacy visible at Monticello. Recognizing this and various thorny historical matters, the current director and Dan Jordan, the immediate past director, were to be congratulated. How easy to deny, dodge, gloss over this fundament to success?

The two cats and dogs discussed the past as people filed in, taking their seats, breaking out little paper fans. Most everyone who was well acquainted with a Virginia summer wore a hat.

The C.O.'s old truck was parked down at the Bowman and Neuhoff house under a shade tree, windows open. The animals had long since slipped away, of course. That Leslie Bowman and Cort Neuhoff didn't care that a beat-up truck was parked among the gleaming BMWs, Mercedes, Jaguars, was a statement in itself. Mr. Jefferson would have approved their egalitarianism.

The cats in the tree could more easily hide than the two dogs. Tucker and Tally, staying quite still, had crawled under nearby thick bushes to observe the proceedings.

"He had a wolf by the ears." Pewter pronounced judgment on Mr. Jefferson's slave owning.

"They all did. Even the North had slaves for a time," Sneaky agreed.

"Why did they get rid of them?" the gray cat wondered.

"I don't know. Too cold, or they were too cheap to feed them. Having a wage slave is a lot more clever. You sell them goods from a company store so they get in hock; if they can't pay for them, you dock their wages. They have to find housing, much of which is owned or was owned by those companies. They pay rent. Right? However you look at it, being poor and powerless is painful," the tiger cat said. "And that's why we have to organize. When we falter in our duties, we're killed, a lot of us. I don't know, maybe that's better than what happened to the humans in the old days. They were left to starve."

"Either way, it sucks," Pewter succinctly replied.

Tally crawled a little closer to get a look.

"Get back here," Tucker ordered. "Someone will see your nose."

Tally wiggled backward. "There are so many people."

Tucker blinked her eyes. "You sure can smell the cheap perfume and cologne."

"Oh, it all smells awful, Tucker. Even the expensive stuff like Creed and Amouage."

They lay next to each other, giggling.

"Our C.O. always worries about money, yet she'll go out and spend hundreds of dollars on that stuff." Tucker sighed.

"That's because they're irrational. I do have to give that to Sneaky Pie. Dogs and cats are a lot more logical. Perfume?" Tally's eyebrows raised. "What about that old lady who collects bone china? I mean, she lives in three rooms full of boxes of this expensive china."

"One of the C.O.'s great-aunts. Did you know some of that china is worth umpteen thousands? Some of it is as old as Monticello."

"What good is it if you don't use it?" the Jack Russell pointedly replied.

"None that I can tell. Bet Mr. J. had fine china." Tucker thought for a moment. "We caught a glimpse of it when we walked through the dining room." The corgi then added, "Wonder if Sneaky Pie is getting nervous?"

"If I stood next to her at the podium, she'd most certainly be cool, calm, and collected." Tally knew she was the best running mate, just knew it.

Noncommittally, Tucker said, "Perhaps."

As welcoming remarks settled the audience, the main speaker followed. Being asked to give the Fourth of July address at Monticello was a singular honor. Presidents may or may not be invited. One couldn't buy one's way into this extraordinary moment, but many tried to use influence to be the main speaker, a mighty boost to a political career. So said the C.O., and Sneaky had been listening closely. The selection process applied more rigorous standards than being elected to public office. In some critical fashion, the human in this position needed to embody the spirit of the Declaration of Independence. In years past, that included military people, members of the judiciary, even entertainers who had been born elsewhere and who had then become U.S. citizens themselves.

Year after year, the main speaker reached out to these new citizens, as well as reaching back to the noble ideals of Mr. Jefferson.

Next, the oath of citizenship was read over the microphone by a high-ranking judge. The applicants stood and agreed to the terms. Each new citizen, name read aloud, mounted the dais, was greeted by those on the dais and given their citizenship papers. Of all annual public ceremonies, the Fourth of July at Monticello may be the most emotional.

Emotional or not, Tally felt the prickle of boredom.

Knowing her friend, Tucker advised, "Be still."

"I'm thirsty," said the Jack Russell.

"You'll have to wait, plus, we have Sneaky Pie's address after this," the wise corgi said.

"Does every single new citizen have to walk across the dais, shake hands, and take a piece of paper?"

Putting her head on her paws, Tucker replied, "They do. Why don't you take a nap?"

"A nap? With all these people? What if someone needs help?"

"I'm sure security is up to the task."

"Security can't chase mice. You know how terrified some people are of mice. And what if a snake slithers out of the garden? There will be panic and mayhem."

"Just rest your mind." Tucker felt this was impossible. Tally fidgeted more by the minute.

"Look at those colors," said the Jack Russell, as she edged closer to the edge of the bush. "Look at that lady. She's beautiful. Look at how the breeze blows her dress. You know, a strong wind could tear her clothes off."

"Tally, that woman is from India. They dress in better colors than our ladies do."

"Yeah, but what if she winds up naked? She'd be so upset."

"I doubt the men would mind." Tucker noticed, as had Tally, that the young lady was exceedingly beautiful, but then, most Indian women are.

After shaking hands with the justice, the woman moved toward the end of the podium and the steps. A stronger puff of wind did lift up the back of her sari, but there were many layers of vibrantly colored thin fabric like gauze.

"I'll save her!"

"Tally, no!" Tucker tried to bite and hold Tally's hind leg, but the little dog wriggled away.

"What the hell?" Sneaky cursed as she watched the rough-coated little monster jump up to the woman as she exited the stage.

"I'll save you," Tally barked.

Fortunately, the brand-new citizen, perhaps twenty-five, liked dogs, so she leaned down to pet Tally, now the center of attention.

"I'm going to be a vice-presidential candidate. I'm going to save America!"

"Not before I kill you first!" Sneaky, enraged, spat so loudly that the birds above her cussed her out.

"I told you she's an idiot," snarled Pewter. "Born an idiot. And she will die an idiot when you kill her, of course." Pewter adopted her all-knowing pose.

Since the dog had no intention of leaving her, the Indian lady scooped up Tally. She returned to her seat, devil dog in her lap, to the cheers of the assembled.

Sneaky saw from her perch, however, that Leslie Bowman was not cheering. The Monticello director recognized the dog, wondered how the animal had snuck into the ceremony, and at that exact moment would have happily throttled the C.O. Steering a national event like this required steady nerves. Fortunately, the director was equal to it.

Leslie's daughter Haley ran down to the house, where the C.O. was putting out centerpieces of red, white, and blue flowers on each small table. Flags flew everywhere, and at each place setting there were, rolled up, small Stars and Stripes.

"Your dog is—" Haley breathlessly began. "She's—" She thought for a moment, hoping to be diplomatic, as her parents had taught her. "Intruded on the ceremony."

"Oh, no." The C.O. immediately followed Haley up the hill.

As the two women trotted, then ran to the back of Monticello, Cort Neuhoff, a medical person, was ministering to a gentleman from Nicaragua whose son had become a citizen. In his excitement to embrace his son, he rose from his chair, then sat down again, because one wasn't to greet family and friends until every single new citizen was back in their seats. Fidgety like Tally, the man stood up again, but slipped and came down, hitting his metal folding chair hard.

"Sneaky, maybe you should wait until next year," Pewter suggested.

"But the presidential election is this year," the tiger cat snapped.

As soon as all were at last pronounced U.S. citizens, everyone stood up, hugging, kissing, and congratulating.

Haley spied the Indian lady surrounded by her parents and friends. Tally was next to her on the ground.

No fool, Tucker stayed away.

"Ma'am, I am so sorry." The C.O.'s face was red. "I think she wanted to congratulate you before anyone else."

"She's adorable," the young woman said in her light, beguiling accent.

The C.O. would have argued that point, but not now. She knelt down, picked up the dog, tucked her under one arm, and with her other hand fished in the pocket of her summer skirt, pulling out a card.

"Ma'am, please call me." She handed the lady her card and addressed her family and friends. Virginia hospitality always made her friends. "Please let me make this up to you all. I would love to have you all out to the farm for a celebration dinner. My friends would be happy to meet you." She paused. "There are a lot of other animals."

They smiled politely. The young woman petted Tally, then hugged the C.O. She was so thrilled to be a new American. "I will," she said.

The people began to walk down and away from Monticello. The citizens and families headed for the director's house. The horses hung their heads over the fence line.

All the way back, the C.O. seemed preoccupied with how she could apologize to Leslie. She met up with Liz Blaine, the right-hand person at Monticello.

Not one iota of shame, Tally greeted her. "Hello, Miss Liz."

Liz couldn't help but laugh. "You're in the doghouse."

Back up at Monticello, the mice emerged from the dome. Some hurried down to a good high spot where they'd have a commanding view of Sneaky's much-anticipated speech. Others, using claws, perched atop the dome. The humans lagging behind the departing crowd didn't notice them.

The birds moved closer, and Art, the Red-shouldered Hawk, had flown up from the farm. Hawks had a large cruising range. Chipmunks appeared. The squirrels sat on tree branches. One by one, dogs had been arriving from the farms surrounding Monticello.

Once the people left, Sneaky and Pewter backed down the tree. Tucker crawled out from the bushes.

The tiger cat raced to the dais and climbed up to the lectern. The microphone was easily swung over the top of the podium, where she now sat.

Sneaky Pie looked out over the assembled animals and began: "We hold these truths to be self-evident, that all living creatures are endowed by their Creator with certain unalienable Rights, that among these are Life, Liberty and the pursuit of Happiness.—That to secure these rights, Governments are instituted among Sentient Creatures, deriving their just powers from the consent of the governed,—That whenever any Form of Government becomes destructive of these ends, it is the Right of the Living to alter or to abolish it, and to institute new Government, laying its foundation on such principles and organizing its powers in such form, as to them shall seem most likely to effect their Safety and Happiness."

The animals listened intently. Not one little peep or squeak punctuated the address.

Sneaky Pie continued: "Friends, on this Fourth of July, I wish to announce my candidacy for the presidency. I promise with the help of Providence to establish and maintain a natural balance between all living creatures: predator and prey. I promise to cherish the earth, the waters, and the air. I cannot promise to end human wars, but I can work mightily to avoid them. I promise hope for the young and comfort for the aged. For all of us in between those two poles, I promise a great common cause, first expressed by the human who lived here: life, liberty, and the pursuit of happiness."

The animals applauded in their individual fashion. This message would be carried, like all great messages, from living creature to living creature. Powerful as the electronic media is in all its forms, nothing great happens without the spark of hope being passed from one creature to another.

Having arrived at her empty truck, the C.O. came searching for the rest of her family, accompanied by the pest Tally herself.

Upon reaching the back of Monticello, Tally raced away, yelling at the top of her lungs "Vice president. I'll make a great vice president."

Sneaky calmly announced to the crowd, "Please take into account that she is a Jack Russell and this is my human. As for a running mate, I have much to consider. I do not, however, think it will be a Jack Russell."

A murmur of approval followed this; the mice especially liked the statement.

The human stopped in her tracks, saw the animals gathered behind her tiger cat at the microphone. Something was occurring, but she couldn't grasp it. She did, however, hear "Meow. Meow."

She noticed the mice on the dome. She looked at the large number of squirrels, birds, and the farm

dogs. She saw the raptor Art near the dais, high in the closest tree. He was a big fellow.

She smiled as she looked around. "I guess we're all Americans celebrating the Fourth of July."

Because the microphone picked up what she had said, a louder murmur followed this, which surprised the C.O.

Looking down at her human, Sneaky said to the gathered masses, "There is hope!"

Campaign Platform

You can check up on me at my website,
   www.catprez.com
or my Facebook page,
   www.facebook.com/sneakypiebrown

I promise never to lie to you.

I promise to reduce the tax burden on humans by utilizing a flat tax and closing all loopholes.

Any human over the age of ninety need not pay federal income taxes.

For animals who have served in the military, I promise pay, retirement pay, and a discount at the veterinarian's office.

For humans I promise they get to deduct veterinary bills.

I promise to work extra hard to see that veterinary schools receive important federal grants for research.

I pledge the use of abandoned federal buildings

for homeless animals. This also includes farmland for abandoned quadrupeds.

I promise federal research money to study the effect of birdsong on human well-being. In England there is such a study at the University of Surrey. We need one here. Humans need emotional help.

In accordance with that need, I will strongly suggest that humans learn about animal languages and needs, beginning in grade school. Respect for all creatures starts young.

Campaign Promises

The centerpiece of my administration will be the responsible use of the environment for all living creatures, and this includes the plant kingdom—they, too, are alive.

Given the state of human mental health, my administration will make every effort to substitute drug therapies with animal companion therapies, even if this means special programs to teach those in need how to care for and live with cats, dogs, horses, birds, et cetera. Anything to get humans off chemical dependencies is a good thing.

I will increase the prestige and the power of the Department of Agriculture, as well as the U.S. Fish and Wildlife Service. If need be, I will work hard to remove overlap, streamline agencies, or collapse competing bureaus into one bureau.

Along with using discarded federal buildings for abandoned animals, I will do the same for abandoned and mistreated children. In my state of Virginia, the best-managed state in the Union (it almost always is), one out of eleven children has slept on the street. This is unforgivable.

I believe in the separation of the church and state, first expressed for the colony of Virginia by James Madison. You practice your faith and I will practice mine.

I will appoint a pack rat to the Federal Reserve. He or she should steady the humans.

I will ensure that humans respect each species' various mating patterns. On this same subject, I will strongly advise most cats and dogs to be neutered or spayed.

I believe any human running for public office at the state and national level should also be neutered or spayed. It will focus the men and calm the women.

I believe we cannot breed past the food and water supply. Population control of all species will be a difficult subject, a challenge to resolve, but we must, and I pledge to begin the discussions.

I promise you I will think clearly. For instance, if a cat has kittens in the oven, that doesn't make them biscuits. I will never try to confuse you with tricky stuff.

I recognize that some predators are more dangerous than others. I will do my best to make appointments that allow for harmony.

For all my Cabinet positions, I will request a veterinary report. For the humans in my Cabinet, I will have the vet check them out, too.

Additional Campaign Information

The Constitution does not specify that only a human can run for the office of president. One must be born a U.S. citizen and be thirty-five years of age or older. I qualify. I am fourteen, which in cat years is older than thirty-five, having been born in Albemarle County, Virginia. I currently live in Nelson County, Virginia.

I need help in my campaign. I am not allowed by law or my publisher to solicit funds. Should you wish to help in any fashion, perhaps be my campaign chair in your state, go to:

www.catprez.com

My Facebook page is www.facebook.com/sneakypiebrown

If all goes well, I will be able to hire Spotted Dog Productions, a mix of canine and human skills, to make weekly videos for you to download on all manner of devices.

Thank you for considering me. Even if I do not become your candidate, please take citizenship seriously. Without your political participation, there will be change, but it probably won't be the change that you would like to see.

Forward,
Sneaky Pie Brown

Rita Mae Brown,
Human Campaign Manager

Tee Tucker,
Canine Campaign Manager

A Note from Rita Mae Brown

You never know. Behind my back, Sneaky Pie wrote out her political manifesto. If you picked up this book expecting a mystery, it's not. Well, life's a mystery, but this is a feline author's desire for a more representative government.

Since I believe the difference between the Republican and Democratic parties is the difference between syphilis and gonorrhea, I have given up. Part of this despair is fueled by what I see in candidates as well as many elected officials: They have exaggerated ideas of their own supremacy, to which minds not normal are especially inclined. Perhaps it was always this way and I now truly see it, or perhaps we are going through a particularly vicious cycle. But I fear nothing much can get done when people or political parties are extremist in views while demonizing all other outlooks. Compromise is possible only between parties, both of which can acknowledge to some extent the force of the other's position.

Therefore I am facing this presidential election with courageous indifference. It's touching that Sneaky Pie is energized. Given all the aggressive banality, I'd settle for competent mediocrity. However, she will not.

Touching though her political program may be, I was unhappy to find myself described herein as the Can Opener, C.O. for short. That cat knows my Christian name perfectly well. Despite this blow to my ego, I was fascinated with how she and the other animals look at what is needed for a good life.

She has a clear vision, not clouded by ideology. She also refuses to engage in religious debate or pressure. This is wise, since it's getting crowded at the foot of the Cross.

With all the detritus of vested interests stripped away, the path does seem clear. The first thing one must take care of is Mother Earth. The next thing one must do is defend one's borders. For Sneaky that always meant her hunting radius, but she now sees beyond that and perhaps farther than I do. She's basic. If you can't work and eat, what good are volumes of legislation about so many incidentals? I'm coming around to her views.

She can't be bought off. I can. I'd like to start with a flawless six-carat emerald-cut diamond, the color of gin and tonic. She's better than I am. Even catnip won't turn her head . . . much.

So she will be my candidate. Not only do I believe in her honesty, I do know that he who denies skimmed milk to the cat must give the mouse cream.

Always and Ever,

Rita Mae Brown / C.O.

Turn the page for an exclusive sneak peek at
Rita Mae Brown and Sneaky Pie Brown's
next Mrs. Murphy Mystery

THE LITTER OF THE LAW

Coming soon in hardcover and eBook from
Bantam Books

When they were courting, Fair Haristeen, doctor of veterinary medicine, would pick up his wife, Harriett—"Harry"—and they'd go on a Saturday drive. He'd be bruised from Friday night's football game. She'd be dirty from the stable. Now in their early forties, they'd steal a Saturday and cruise the back roads in central Virginia.

Mrs. Murphy, the tiger cat, Pewter, her gray, overweight sidekick, and Tucker, the corgi, looked out the window from the backseat. The three animal friends usually accompanied their people everywhere except in high heat. On a day like today, windows down a crack, the three could sleep or chat while the humans talked.

"Perfect," Fair replied.

October 12 proved a ravishing fall day, early fall, for the summer warmth lingered late this year. The forest looked spray-painted with yellow, orange, flaming red, deep red, old gold.

"Hey, Miranda got the respiratory flu." Harry

mentioned a former co-worker and dear friend. "She's swearing that drinking electrolytes will cure her. She saw it on TV."

"We've got plenty of quacks now." Fair grimaced. He shook his head. "Electrolytes will help, but our beloved Miranda seems susceptible to quacks."

Watching the passing scenery, the cat Pewter noticed a lovely yellow clapboard farmhouse. "*Quack. Duck. Why call a crook a quack?*"

"*I don't know,*" Tucker replied. The corgi was well-used to Pewter's inquiring mind. "*They also use the term* snake oil. *A quack sells snake oil. It's confusing.*"

"Ha." Pewter let out a whoop. "*If they'll buy snake oil, maybe we can get our human hooked on catnip.*"

"*She won't sniff catnip,*" Tucker replied with dignity. Someone had to stand up for Harry.

"*They can learn,*" the gray cat spoke with conviction.

"*Pewter, sometimes I think you're cracked as well as fat,*" the dog unwisely said.

"*Fat?*" Pewter raged.

"*You need a seat all your own. Every time we take a turn the flab on your belly sways.*" Tucker growled.

Pewter lashed out, a quick right to the shoulder.

Tucker growled, showing her fangs.

"That is enough!" Harry turned around.

"*I haven't done a thing,*" Mrs. Murphy said, distancing herself from the combatants, who then rounded on her.

"*Brown noser!*" Pewter whacked the tiger cat, who gave as good as she got.

The hissing and barking irritated Fair to the point where he drove to the side of the road near Hester Martin's vegetable and fruit stand.

Harry got out of the car, opened the back door. "I am going to give you such a smack."

All three animals jumped to the far back of the Volvo station wagon. She opened that back lift so they jumped into their original seats.

Slamming the back door, Harry cursed as Fair couldn't help but laugh. She walked over to the driver's side; he had the window down. "They know how to pluck your last nerve," Fair said, laughing.

"Yours, too. I didn't pull the car over." Harry looked down the road at the produce stand, a small white clapboard building with a large overhang, goods displayed in orderly, colorful rows. "Hey, let's get some pattypan squash. Bet Hester still has some." She walked around, getting in the car's passenger side before turning to face her animal tormentors. "If I hear one peep, one sniff, one hiss while I am shopping, no food tonight. Get it?"

"*Hateful.*" Pewter turned her back on Harry.

As Tucker hung her head, Mrs. Murphy, the tiger cat, loudly defended herself. "*I didn't do one thing.*"

"*Of course not, the perfect puss.*" Pewter curled her upper lip.

Fair coasted the car to the stand where Hester—wearing an orange apron, black jeans, and an orange shirt—talked to customers, most of whom lived in Crozet or nearby.

"I'll stay here." Fair knew how Hester could go on, plus Buddy Janss was there, all three hundred pounds of him, and he could outtalk Hester.

Orange and black bunting festooned the roof overhang. Scarecrows flanked the outdoor wooden cartons overflowing with squashes, pumpkins, every kind of apple imaginable. Inside one could buy a good ham and cheese sandwich. Little ghosts floated from the rafters, big green eyes glowed in the room's upper corners. Brilliantly gold late corn, huge mums, and zinnias added to the color.

A sign, almost as big as Buddy, sat catty-cornered to the entrance, announcing the community Halloween Hayride to raise money for the Crozet Library. No doubt Tazio Chappars, an architect, designed the impressive sign. She worked hard for the library and the sign really grabbed you: from a large drawn skeleton, one bony arm actually reached out to get your attention.

Hester looked up. "Harry Haristeen, I haven't seen you in weeks."

Buddy turned. "How'd you do with your sunflowers?"

Buddy, a farmer who rented thousands of acres along with his own holdings, enjoyed getting reports about Harry's foray into niche farming. Who knew better than Buddy the cost of equipment and implements for wheat, corn, soybeans? Harry knew she'd made a wise choice in focusing on sunflowers, as well as a quarter acre of petite manseng grapes and ginseng down by the creek which divided her property from the old Jones farm.

"Pretty good," she said, not wanting to brag that this year's yield of sunflowers was her biggest yet. "How's your year so far?"

He hooked his thumbs in his overalls. "Tell you what, girl, that mini drought thinned out my corn crop. I did better than most because my lower acres got enough rain, others didn't. Never saw anything like it. On one side of the road the corn would be twisted right up, and on the other just as plump as you'd please. Lost most of the corn behind the old school houses."

Hester jumped in. "Government's fault. All that stuff they have circling around up there in space. Gotta affect us."

Both Harry and Buddy nodded politely, for Hester was a little in space herself. Sometimes she was way out there. Middle-aged, with glossy light brown hair hanging to her shoulders, she applied just enough makeup to draw attention to her healthy good looks. Every small town as well as big cities have Hesters; it's just they can't hide in the small towns. Good-looking people, often bright, but they don't quite fit in and often they never marry. Hester had gone to Mary Baldwin College, excelled in her studies, but came back over the Blue Ridge Mountains to run this roadside stand. Her parents had built it more as a hobby than a business but it flourished. Her father had been a banker. Her mother ran the stand. She seemed happy enough, engaged with a steady stream of regulars, classmates, and tourists.

Buddy kindly semi-agreed. "What scares me is what we don't know. I mean just in general, look at this drought and hey, we came out a lot better off than they did in the Midwest where everything burned up. Right now our water table is good. I planted more corn because I think it will stay warm longer. I'll get it harvested and, if not, I'll make a lot of critters happy." He let out a booming laugh.

Hester asked, "You've got crop coverage, Buddy? After the drought of 1988, surely you started paying for an insurance policy, revenue protection."

"I do. I elected an eighty-percent revenue protection policy. Yes, I did learn from 1988 but, girl, every time I turn around I'm writing another check and I see my return diminish. Farming gets harder and harder," said the well-organized man, a true steward of the land. "Just to keep up I have to plant more acreage. Plant an early crop, then come back and throw soybeans down. I feel like I'm running to stay in place."

"Think we all do," Hester agreed.

"Only way I can buy or rent, and renting makes sense in the short term, is to sell some of my land closer in to Crozet or Charlottesville."

Hester's shoulders snapped back. "Don't do that, Buddy. Don't ever do that."

Harry didn't want to keep Fair or the arguing animals waiting. "Before I forget, Hester, do you have any pattypan squash?"

"I do. Wait until you see it." Hester nodded to Buddy, who winked at Harry.

The two women walked inside where there was a

gorgeous array of crookneck squash, acorn squash, and Harry's favorite: cream white pattypan squash that looked like scalloped discuses.

"Beautiful! And the right size."

"Right about now the pattypan is usually over, but with this year's long, long summer, still getting some. The melons are over though." Hester thoughtfully replied, "I do so love melons. Before I forget now, you and Fair are buying tickets for the hayride. You must. The library is built but there's a lot to be done. We need $59,696 just for adult computers and, oh my, the adult area needs tables and we need furniture for a quiet reading room. The list is endless."

"Of course, we'll buy tickets. I'll even buy tickets for Mrs. Murphy, Pewter, and Tucker."

"If that gray cat of yours gets any fatter, I'll have to find a special wagon and pony just for her." Hester laughed.

"You're looking pretty Halloweeny yourself, all orange and black."

"Oh, this is just my warm-up. Next week I'll be out here in my witch's costume."

"So long as you don't scare customers away."

"I could be a Halloween fairy except I've never seen a Halloween fairy."

They laughed as Harry picked out two succulent

squashes, and paid at the cash register run by Lolly Currie. Harry knew the ambitious young woman was looking for a better-paying job, but making ends meet at the fruit stand until then.

Back on the road, Fair grinned. "That was the shortest time you have ever spent at Martin's stand."

"Buddy Janss helped me out because as soon as I paid for my squash, he came back to chat up Hester, about late produce deliveries. I swear, Buddy has put on more weight. His chins now have chins."

"Buddy may be fat but he's light on his feet. He was a hell of a football player in high school and college. It's a pity but retired linemen run to fat so often."

"Boxers, too." She watched rolling hills pass by.

"*Maybe you should go live with Buddy Janss,*" said Tucker, knowing this would cause a fight. "*The two of you could be Team Tubby.*"

"*Don't.*" Mrs. Murphy counseled in vain.

"*Bubble butt. Poop breath!*" Pewter hissed loudly.

Harry twisted around in the front seat just in time to see Pewter hook the dog's shoulder with one claw.

"*Ouch,*" she yelped.

"*Next. Your eyes.*"

279

"Pull over, honey," said Harry. "There will be fur all over the car if I don't stop this right now."

He pulled over on the two-lane road which ran into Garth Road. The north field was jammed with corn. Morrowdale Farm usually put these fields in good hay but this year row after row of healthy corn filled them and they had somehow escaped the small drought.

Opening the door to again castigate the backseat passengers, Harry remarked, "This has to be one of the best run and prettiest farms in Albemarle County."

"Sure is."

They looked out to the scarecrow in the middle of the field, currently being mobbed by crows.

"I thought scarecrows frightened crows?" Fair shrugged.

"Those crows are having a party. Look at that. Pulling on the wig under the hat." Harry laughed. "What are all those birds doing?"

Fair stepped out of the car to stare intently as a crow plucked out an eyeball.

"Honey, that's not a scarecrow," he said.